THE CASE OF THE YELLOW DIAMOND

THE CASE OF THE YELLOW DIAMOND

Carl Brookins

NORTH STAR PRESS OF ST. CLOUD, INC.
St. Cloud, Minnesota

Printed in the United States of America

Published by
North Star Press of St. Cloud, Inc.
P.O. Box 451
St. Cloud, Minnesota 56302

northstarpress.com

CHAPTER 1

THE GUY SPRAWLED on my office floor was dead. I didn't need my years of experience as a private snoop to know that. The big bloody hole in his bare chest clued me in. The recently deceased was about seventy, I judged, and portly, overweight, even. He was a white man wearing expensive sandals and what was probably an upscale pair of boxer-style swimming trunks. They looked dry, but I didn't touch them to verify that. I sniffed. The blood smell was strong and the dark pool under his right shoulder was just starting to congeal. I didn't smell any gunpowder. I recognized him, of course.

I stepped carefully around the body to avoid getting blood on my favorite tennis shoes and picked up my recently acquired cell phone to dial 911. After that I called my friend Ricardo Simon, an experienced investigator with the Minneapolis PD. I sometimes talked with him about puzzling aspects of my cases. I wasn't your typical taciturn PI who viewed every cop as a potential enemy. I was atypical in a lot of ways. I often wore red Converse, for example. The ones with white soles.

"Detective Simon," he answered.

"Sean," I said. "You remember my case involving diamond smuggling?"

"Of course."

"My principal suspect's dead. In my office. Large-caliber gunshot to the upper chest."

"Preston Pederson? Wow. Did you kill him?"

"No, I just found him."

"Call 911?"

"Of course."

Ricardo hummed for a few seconds, then said, "Appears you'll have to revisit your case while reordering your thinking. Hmm. Stay in touch."

1

"Thanks," I said and clicked off. This case was getting more and more complicated.

The case to which I refered started a few weeks ago in a suburb of Saint Paul. Actually, the case started years ago, in a previous century and about six thousand miles to the west. But I'm getting ahead of myself.

* * * *

Living in a suburb of the twin cities of Minneapolis and Saint Paul isn't always easy; dying—almost anywhere—on the other hand, can be a cinch. I grew up here, so I knew the idiosyncrasies of each city, the upsides as well as the downsides. Minneapolis, the larger of the two towns (twins they have never been), is the gray, solid, businessman kind of city. Urban renewal is a big part of their scene. The streets are laid out in a rectangular grid using a logical, repetitive pattern: avenues alphabetical east to west, streets in numerical sequence starting somewhere near the center of the city and running north and south. Sure, there are variations due to topography and the idiosyncrasies of developers. But not many.

Saint Paul, on the other hand, is a series of streets and avenues with a few boulevards tossed in that seem to wander about at random. In the central part of the city there are numbered streets and named avenues, not to mention a few "places." But labels quickly change to lanes, names, and boulevards. I'm a native, grew up and went to high school in the system, and even *I* get lost from time to time. But now I live in Roseville, a suburb on the north side of the metro area, and have an office in Minneapolis. I still consider Saint Paul home. So does the post office, for that matter.

So what, you may be asking, has this to do with anything? To be truthful, nothing at all. I was trying to find my way to an address on the east side of St. Paul, over near Lake Phalen, about ten miles east of where I live in a straight line. Except you can't hardly go in a straight line, east to west, so I got lost. St. Paul's like that. Every so often it'll rise up and bite you.

Being lost, I was late for my appointment. By pure luck, I found my way to the Phalen corridor and realized I was only a few blocks from the new State Bureau of Criminal Apprehension building. I had a friend there, a national expert on DNA analysis. That's what she worked on in their lab.

That and old cases. It was helpful having friends and acquaintances in important positions who could ease my way through this life. Down the hall from my office was another office where good friends were ensconced, folks who knew everything there was to know about computers and how to use or misuse the Internet. One might think of them as hackers. They knew how to search digitally, penetrate and leave no trace. They were not, as far as I knew, affiliated with any government agency.

More and more today, private investigation involves telephone and computer searching. As personal privacy disappears, more and more investigators use the Internet to find the information they needed. Me, I prefered personal contact. Eyeball to eyeball, as it were. I was far from being an expert computer/Internet user. When I had the need, my friends down the hall, the Revulon sisters, did computer dances for me. They're big, blonde Scandinavian women, a heck of a lot easier on the eyes than any computer screen. The Revulons sort of adopted me. They knew my live-in significant girlfriend, Catherine Mckerney, and approved. I suppose it's more accurate to say I was the live-in because Catherine and I spend most of our downtime together at her place, a very nice, large apartment in an upscale part of Minneapolis, instead of at my nice split-level in Roseville.

So what does all this have to do with anything? It's by way of an introduction to me, my piece of life on this planet and a case that recently came my way. The case started many years earlier and a long way away. It began near a small, insignificant speck of dirt and coral in the middle of the Pacific Ocean. Now, I'm sure the speck of land isn't insignificant to the people who lived there, or those who died there. But if I ask someone, "Have you ever heard of Yap Island?" chances are the answer would be no. Unless you happen to be a student of that large war in the world that happened in the last century. In particular, what they called the Pacific Theater of that war. Parenthetically, it has always amazed me that the Pacific Theater was so named, because, like the ocean, it wasn't very. Pacific, that is.

* * * *

THE LARGE WAR, OFFICIALLY called World War Two, happened between Germany, Italy, and Japan on one side, and just about everybody else, including the U.S. of A, on the other. There was the European Theater and the afore-mentioned Pacific Theater, although there wasn't a lot of acting in either the-ater. It was mostly fighting and dying. A general named MacArthur got tossed out of the Pacific after the Imperial Japanese Army overran the Philip-pine Islands. That was just after the Imperial Japanese Navy air wing wiped out a significant part of the American Navy at Pearl Harbor, which is in the Islands of Hawaii, also in the Pacific and now our fiftieth state. Then it was merely one of our territories.

That's enough history, except to note that General MacArthur, with the help of a few Marines and the U.S. Navy, did return to the Philippines. Along the way there were several scraps at, around, and over various islands and segments of empty Pacific Ocean. One of those islands was a pinprick on the map, an atoll named Yap.

I had never heard of Yap Island until a guy walked into my office one fine morning and plunked down in my side chair, the one bolted to the floor. It gave Tod Bartelme a bit of a jolt when he couldn't use his finely sculpted arms to move the chair. I could see it in his face. Here was a man who clearly worked out to keep his body well tuned. He frowned and gave up after two tries to move the chair. I had the chair bolted down so irate clients didn't try to throw it at me. My friend, Minneapolis Police Detective Ricardo Simon, insisted the chair was bolted down so it was always in direct range of the pistol strapped to the underside of my desk. Totally untrue. There's no pistol strapped to the under-side of my desk. It's actually a used sawed-off, single-barreled shotgun.

Sarcasm, my lover, Catherine Mckerney, sometimes remarked, would one day get me a fat lip. So far, I've been able to dodge that event. On my slender, five-foot-plus frame, a fat lip would look unfortunate. Oh, I've received a fat lip or two in my line of work, but not for sarcasm.

Anyway, Tod Bartelme. He's the dude who showed up, exuding health, a super positive attitude, and a problem. He was alone, tall and wor-ried, and he said so after we'd gotten through the obligatory introductions and he'd settled into that visitor's chair.

"What are you worried about?" I queried. I tried to zero in on the main issues as quickly as I could. Otherwise, we can waste a lot of time, and time, as somebody once said, is money. I don't quite follow that reasoning, but there you go.

"It all started three Christmases ago. Traditionally, the family, well, my wife's family, insists we all get together for the holidays. So after dinner Christmas Day, we were all sitting around the living room relaxing, having a little Christmas cheer, watching a little football. You know."

He gestured. I nodded.

"Anyway my wife Josie—her name is Jocelyn but we all call her Josie—Josie mentions she's been taking a noncredit course from some extension operation at the U, the Osher Lifelong Learning Institute. Everybody calls it Ollie. Don't ask me why."

I hadn't been planning to do so.

"Josie says it's a history course on World War Two. The Pacific Theater part."

"Ah," I said. "The Solomon Islands, Okinawa, Bataan, places like that. The Battle of Midway." I may be short but I do have a little education.

Bartelme gave me a look and nodded. "Yeah, that's right. There's another island out there that figured in the war. It's named Yap. It belonged to the Japanese after the First World War and they built an airstrip and buildings and some other stuff. It's about six hundred miles east from Japan."

"Six hundred miles. Round trip, twelve hundred. A bomber could just make it, but fighters don't carry enough gas, I betcha."

Tod Bartelme looked a little surprised. "You know about these things?"

"Only recently learned," I said. "When you called for this appointment and said you wanted to talk about Yap Island, I did a little checking since I'd never heard of the place. It sounds like a location a married man or woman might go to get away from a family problem."

Bartelme shook his head and smiled. "Maybe, but that's not the situation here." He went on to explain that his wife's granduncle had been a flyer in the war and was lost somewhere in the vicinity of this Yap Island. Shot down. The bodies of the crew had never been recovered, nor had those of the crews of two other bombers in the flight that went down in the same action. "Josie got it in her head she'd like to see the place her granduncle was lost. She said when she chatted with her sister Julie about maybe going out there, she started wondering about that part of the world and what happened there. So she asked her relatives about it, and the story came out. Part of it, anyway."

"When Josie gets an idea in her head, it most often happens," said Tod.

CHAPTER 2

TOD BARTELME TOLD ME a lot of other things, too. About how he and Josie were experienced SCUBA divers and that it looked like the bomber with her granduncle shot down over Yap went into the ocean with everybody aboard. The wreck had never been found. A sad story, but it had happened to a lot of others and it happened a long time ago, and I wasn't so sure I needed to know all that. I still wasn't clear on why the Bartelmes needed the services of a private investigator located in Minneapolis, Minnesota. So I interrupted my potential client to ask, "This is all interesting history, Mr. Bartelme. But I confess I don't see the connection to today. Why do you want to hire me?"

Bartelme stopped and took a swig from a water bottle he carried. He smiled. "Sorry. I'll get to the point. It appears someone's trying to sabotage our next trip to Yap."

"Sabotage. Your trip to Yap." Of all the things I might have supposed Bartelme would say, that was about at the end of the list. Hell, it didn't even make it *on* the list. "Somebody doesn't want you to go back to the South Pacific? Why?"

"Haven't a clue. That's where you come in, if you'll take the case, Mr. Sean."

I liked that he didn't hesitate over my name. Over either of my names. My first name was the same as my last. Sean Sean, Private Investigator, Ltd. That was what it says on my office door. I had it painted there when I leased this office. I might be limited in the height department, being only five-two, but otherwise, I was fully functional.

I didn't do divorce cases or other domestic wrangles, and I tried to stay away from the bent-nose boys, the organized, mobbed up, fellows. I had an acquaintance, a guy in town who was a player. Maybe. I don't believe everything he told me. He claimed to have some ties to organized crime in places like Chicago. I used him as a sort of resource. If I got vibes I didn't like, he could often warn me if I was getting too close to an organized felony. I used to insist I'd never get involved with the CIA and international spies and such, but then last year I had to deal with a stolen painting. From Poland.

Tod Bartelme was not mobbed up and he wasn't a wise guy. From everything I could determine with a quick Internet search, he was just a guy who had worked for the state in mid-level administrative positions for a ton of years and had never been in any trouble with the law. I hadn't met his family, but that could come later. Right now I had to suss out whether there was even a case here. We talked some more and I made some notes. Then we made an appointment for the coming weekend. I would drive to their place on White Bear Lake, a northeastern outer suburb of Saint Paul. I wasn't fond of woods and brush and things rural, even though I lived in an inner suburb with a lot of trees. A former client gave me the place. I could hardly refuse, right? I grew up in the city and I liked it there. I even enjoyed the tall buildings, the smell of hot pavement in the summer, the street musicians, the parties and even the scufflers and the players. Some of them. The Bartelmes liked the cooler leafier suburban life. And the water. Okay with me.

What I'd learned from Tod that made me think there was something hinky going on was this: for a couple of years Josie and Tod have been looking for her granduncle, Richard Terry Amundson. The Bartelmes had done their research and even made two trips to Yap. They had zeroed in on his bomber group, the planes and the date and approximate flight route. They had developed a contact with a guy in St. Louis who said he was a crew member of a different aircraft in the same group and could tell them things. What things? Important things, apparently. He was due to arrive in the Twin Cities a few days after my meeting with the Bartelmes.

Bartelme was excited. He explained he thought that, with the information the St. Louis vet would supply, they'd pinpoint more precisely the location of the bomber when it was shot down. That was to be their next big trip, coming up in August.

But then, he said, things started going wrong. Oddly wrong. "Suddenly, the wheels are coming off the cart," as he put it. Somebody seemed determined he and his wife should not go back to the remote island of Yap or ever find her granduncle's remains. Would I meet with him and his wife to discuss the rash of odd happenings?

Yes, I would meet with them. I was willing to meet because what little I had learned about Yap and the war in the Pacific intrigued me. I also had a personal connection, tenuous though it was. What I knew of my dad was what my mother had told me not long before she died. My dad had been in the service, probably the Navy, although my mom wasn't too clear when the topic came up. He'd definitely been in the Pacific, she told me, fighting the North Koreans. I'd never met my dad. He and my mom had split right after I showed up. Her information about his sojourn in the service was sketchy. She also told me that my grandfather, her dad, had been in the service as well. He was apparently a sailor and had been in action in the Pacific. I'd never met my grandfather, either. I was intrigued, mildly so, by Bartelme's tale. So I'd journey out to the far eastern reaches of our metropolitan area, to that foreign land called White Bear Lake, to meet his wife and look over the information they had. Then I'd assess the problems that had recently poked up and see what there was to be seen.

Meanwhile, but not back at some ranch, I would connect with my pard, and we'd ride off to some nice downtown restaurant for the evening repast before we took in a late movie or something else just as benign.

* * * *

MY PARDNER IS THE TALL, willowy and wealthy massage therapist Catherine Mckerney, holder of profitable massage contracts and owner of a massage therapy school and a bunch of stocks. Her dad had left Catherine well-enough fixed, but being a smart cookie and not one to rest on her well-formed backside, she bought a massage school and turned a documented need into a lucrative operation that gave her a very comfortable living, something I was willing and able to share.

What? Shocked? I made a reasonable living as an independent PI. I shuffled about and took care of business just fine. But there was no fancy mansion on Lake of the Isles, no Bentley in the garage. No Pontiac GTO, for that matter. I had my little office on Central Avenue, and I had my practice, and as long as Catherine Mckerney would put up with my short-comings and my demented wit, we had a fine relationship. It's called love, I think.

I wheeled into the underground garage at Catherine's abode, then zipped up to the fourth floor and down the well-carpeted hall to our apartment. As I went I admired the fine prints on the walls between doors. The doors were widely spaced because the apartments on the fourth floor were roomy, sporting multiple bed- and other rooms. Catherine liked her space, and as I might have mentioned, whatever Catherine likes . . .

Inside, I discovered I was alone save for the blinking light on our joint telephone service. I was something of a reluctant techno user. I had a regular "blower" in my office, one of those units that squatted on a desk. With wires hooking it to the wall. It had a letter and number dial, and you picked up the hand piece and talked into one end while listening to the other. There was an extension here in Catherine's place and another in my Roseville palace, my address of record. Catherine had a cell phone. I owned one but most emphatically did not carry it. Who wanted to talk on the telephone while driving somewhere? Not me. Maybe I was prejudiced because, not that long ago, I helped an EMT after a bad multi-car accident on a freeway at the edge of the city. I had the misfortune to help collect body parts. One of the parts we collected was the hand and wrist of one of the three dead drivers. The fingers still clutched a cell phone.

So, with the telephone arrangement, I knew I could answer the blinking summons because it was *our* telephone service. I picked up the mobile unit and ambled into the kitchen while I retrieved the call. There was only one. It was my sultry-voiced lover, Catherine herself.

"I miss you, sweetie. And I have to postpone tonight's dinner date. Some things at the school need my immediate attention. I'll make it up to you. There are leftovers in the fridge. I should be home by eleven or so and then we'll have some fun." Her voice dropped almost an octave, and she sort of growled at me when she hung up. It was very stimulating.

Before Catherine and I came together after a chance meeting at a symphony ball affair, I would have gone out for a quick supper or back to my office with a beer and brat takeout. Something like that. Catherine had modified my eating habits so I was healthier. I checked the refrigerator, went and changed and slipped down to the basement pool to do a few laps. After laps, supper consisted of a large plate of cold broiled chicken, a bowl of cole slaw and a very nice crisp Sterling Sauvignon Blanc. The Napa Valley variety.

Later, about eleven-forty or so, just as I was dozing off after having watched Charlie Rose interview somebody important, the other side of our big bed sank a bit and a long-legged, naked siren slid under the covers and began making free with my body.

CHAPTER 3

NOON, ON A SUNNY summer day in Minneapolis. Well-rested, well-sated and rarin' to go, I left my office where I'd checked my mail and messages and headed east for my meeting with Tod and Josie Bartelme.

Half an hour later, I wheeled my tired blue Taurus into a wide, winding driveway of slick-looking asphalt and up to an even wider turn-around and parking area. On the right stood a white three-stall garage. It looked to have a big room over the stalls. Directly ahead was a large fieldstone-walled house with windows set back from the façade in rock sills and neat wood frames. I exited from my ride and took a gander at the three-story home. It was pretty obvious this was the back of the house, which was oriented to the other side. I expected that would be the lakeside. I was right.

An ordinary door at the side appeared to provide access to a narrow space between garage and house. The breezeway door between the garage and the side of the house opened and a teenaged blond boy grinned out at me. "Hi," he said in a high tenor. "I'm Cal. Pederson. You must be Mr. . . . Sean."

"I am," I replied. I walked toward him and we shook hands. Kid seemed mature and self-possessed for one I judged to be about sixteen. He had me in the height department by an inch or so.

"Your first and last names are the same. That's sorta odd, isn't it?"

"It is. My mother did that. But I don't mind. I'm used to it."

"Cool. My name's actually Calvin. I don't like it much so everybody calls me Cal. Or Buddy. You're a PI? A private investigator?"

"Right."

"Cool. D'you carry a gun?"

"Almost never." I gave him a sideways glance as he pointed me into the breezeway and toward another door facing west, this one up two steps. We went through the door and into a large room with a slanted ceiling. Half a cathedral. The wall facing me several yards away was all glass. It looked out on a shady lawn and farther away, the lake. We came in at one end and under a balcony, which was an extension of the second floor where I guessed the bedrooms were. I stepped out from under the balcony and glanced up. Apparently all the second-floor rooms looked at the glassed wall as well. Nice. The kid kept up a steady stream of chatter, and I learned he was Josie and Tod's nephew, that he was from Chicago, and was staying with his aunt and uncle for the summer.

I heard voices in murmured conversation. "Everybody's waiting on the deck," said Cal, pointing toward a sliding glass door at one end of the opposite wall. The fourth wall held a large fieldstone fireplace that looked clean but well used and two doors in the wood-paneled wall. Turned out the deck extended a few more feet along the axis of the glass wall. The deck held a long white table and lots of chairs. Several people looked up or stood when they saw us coming. It was, apparently, a gathering of the clan Pederson or Bartelme. I'd expected to meet privately with just Tod and Josie. This affair looked to be a command performance of some sort.

If I'd realized that, I would have created a powerpoint presentation. Not that I had any idea how to do so. Or how to run one. We ambled through the glass door at one side of the room and Cal led me soberly toward the assembled family. He was clearly delighted to be presenting me to his family unit.

Apart from Tod Bartelme and Cal, of course, I recognized only one other person. He was a tall, stork-like man, someone I'd encountered in an oblique way in the past. He was a lawyer who specialized in trusts, retirement investments, money management, wills, and conveyances—things that I have only limited understanding of or contact with. That was due to my lack of loose cash. His name was Anderson. Gareth Anderson. Gary, he was called. Slender, six-six or -seven with a carefully barbered, short, ginger mustache and head of hair, he had a sharp penetrating gaze which belied his smile and easygoing manner. I reached up and shook his hand since he was closest. I wondered why he was present at this preliminary meeting.

Calvin nudged my arm then and steered me to a nicely set-up woman with short brown hair, an amused expression on her lips, and a slender, athletic-looking body. This was Cal's aunt, Josie Pederson Bartelme, wife of Tod. I knew she was a lawyer with a Saint Paul firm, but that was about all I'd had time to learn. She had a strong, almost-hard grip and when she turned to take a chair, I could see the fluidity of movement and athletic economy that a diver would naturally possess.

Preston Pederson was next, father of Josie, head of the clan, if I was any judge. I knew a little about him, just from reading the local newspapers. The old man still moved well, if slowly. He had been a vigorous, perhaps even a dominating personality in his younger years. Preston had built a solid business in the investment field on the foundation of his father's development and construction firm. He was one of the Twin Cities movers and shakers. His eyes were cold and appraising, and he held my hand in another hard grip a little longer than necessary. His smile was wide and generous. "I think you should know," he said after the introduction, "that you weren't our first choice."

I raised one eyebrow, something I occasionally practice in the mirror, to signify I wasn't put off by his statement. Behind him I caught a fleeting grimace from Tod. "Well, Mr. Pederson, I'm here now, so we'll all just have to make the best of the circumstance, won't we?"

He shrugged minimally and stepped back to find a chair at the table. I felt that little tingle that usually told me I was committed. Later I wondered if he was playing me, that he'd wanted me to have that reaction.

Oily showed up next in the form of one Alvin Pederson. Family characteristics weren't his strong suit. I never got the exact family connection. A cousin, perhaps? Weak of chin and shifty of eye, his handshake was nevertheless normal. He was slender and, unlike the rest of the men present, dressed in a suit over a blue dress shirt with a paisley tie snugged up. He looked hot and uncomfortable. Then came sex. A lot of it and pretty blatant.

Introduced as Alvin's wife, this was Maxine. I was nonplussed for a moment. I recovered quickly without outward sign, I hoped, but I caught my breath when she inhaled. She did that a lot. Her tight white tennis dress showed off her impressive cleavage. The short skirt showed off her well-shaped, tanned legs to good advantage as well. She was easily ten years younger than her husband. Her eyes, wide-spaced and dark brown, were as active as I'd ever seen. She scanned me side to side, and up and down as well. It was a quick assessment, and I'd bet she had my net worth within a few hundred, one way or the other. Her hands were quick and agile. She didn't shake my hand, but took me by the arm. She came close, touched my shoulder, and one hand ran up, then down my arm. If we'd been alone, I figured she'd have squeezed my biceps and made oohing and ahhing noises. It all took just seconds. When she turned to release me back to the rest of the assemblage, she leaned in just enough so I felt her breast slide along my upper arm. I resisted an urge to check and see if my wallet was still in place.

When I looked beyond the voluptuous Maxine at the rest of the folks, a couple of the men appeared bemused or maybe envious. Josie Bartelme looked a little uncomfortable, as if she thought Maxine's come-on out of place.

"Come and sit down, Mr. Sean. Would you like something to drink?" asked Josie.

"Thank you, no. I'm fine. I'd like to get to the meat of the matter, as it were, and have you folks tell me just what it is I can do for you this day." I already had a good idea what I could do for, or to, the lot of them. The vibrations were beginning to get me in the pit of the old stomach. I was starting to assume I'd need a drink before this war kicked off.

There was a general shuffling about as people found chairs. Alvin sat on my left, just behind Josie Bartelme. His wife, Maxine, wobbled off on her high heels to the far end of the oval table where she sank gracefully into the shade of an umbrella-ed lounger, a bored expression settling on her face.

Preston Pederson, Pres to his friends, of whom there were few, according to one of my sources, sat in the chair close on my right and dragged it noisily closer so he was almost in my space. Figured. He was, after all, the moneyman in this group. Neither of the Bartelmes held high-income jobs that would support multiple diving trips to Yap Island. Alvin looked like he poured most of his disposable income down his throat and onto his wife's shapely back. At the last minute another man stepped out of the house onto the patio. He introduced himself as an associate of Preston Pederson. I took him to be a hard man who would sometimes be called on to do hard things for his employer.

"So, Mr. Sean. What is it you can do for us?" The question came, as I'd expected, from Preston Pederson. Tod had opened his mouth and then closed it again. "Sorry, Tod, I know this is your show, I just thought I'd get the ball rolling."

"Depends on what you want." Tod and I had already had this conversation, but I addressed him directly. Regardless of where the money came from, I figured it was his deal until he told me different. "As I understand it, you're embarked on another somewhat perilous effort to get to the South Pacific to try to locate a drowned B-24 off Yap Island. You're looking for a missing relative. A granduncle, I believe?"

"That's right, Mr. Sean. My granduncle Richard Amundson flew with the 350th Bomber Wing during the war. He was stationed in the Pacific in Hawaii first and then they moved to a forward base." Smoothly, his wife Josie picked up the narration.

"Later when U. S. and British forces, along with help from Australia, began to overrun the islands the Japanese had fortified, the bomber group was relocated farther to the west in order to bomb the Japanese mainland on a regular basis. They were also used to support the invasions of the Pacific islands, like Iwo Jima."

She stopped and Tod took up the tale. This was something these two obviously did for some sort of public presentations and they fell naturally into their practiced roles. "In July of 1944, Josie's granduncle was in a four-plane group that flew from a base on Los Negros to Saipan. My records aren't entirely clear as to the target of that raid. On the way home the bombers were attacked by a number of Zeroes out of the airstrip at Yap." He stopped when I raised an eyebrow at him.

"Zeroes?" he grinned. "Our designation for one of the Japanese little single-seat fighter airplanes.

"I guess the bombers had slipped by on the way out in the dark, but now it was broad daylight for their return flight. So apparently they were easy targets. Three of the four planes were shot down and crashed in the ocean. Josie's granduncle was on one of them."

Tod stopped and took a breath. Except for birds twittering in nearby bushes, we were silent. It had happened almost seventy years ago, but talking about armed action in skies over that distant ocean and involving the death of a relative seemed to bring it rushing back in all its immediacy. Young men in the ferocity of their potent youth, struggling for what they believed in, for what they knew to be true and right, directed into combat by old soldiers who were a lot less certain of the right or wrong of it. *Combat,* I thought. *The fog of war.* I had never experienced it and had never had a desire to do so. In spite of my profession, I wasn't so sure the force of arms was the best way to settle things. Ever.

In the near silence, Josie got up and went to the rail facing the water, her head turned away. White Bear Lake was blue and quiet in the sun. Tod glanced at his wife and then resumed in a softer voice.

"Anyway, Amundson went down and is still listed with the others in his crew as MIA, missing in action. After we got interested in his history, we—Josie, actually—did a lot of research. Then two years ago we went to Yap and, using the records we had found, dove where we thought the bombers might be. It's not that deep in a lot of places and we located a plane. Not the right one, but we were sure we were on the right track."

"The plane you found was one of those in the mission you were looking for? What sort of research did you do?" I asked.

"Internet, the library, lots of reading. It's pretty interesting, actually," Josie turned back to us and said. "Then I had the idea to contact any members of the bomber wing who were still alive. The VA and some private organizations helped me find people."

"We have a lot of letters," said Tod.

"I'd like to see some of them," I said.

Tod nodded and went on. "Well, we were thinking about whether we could make another trip out there. It's a long way and expensive."

"How'd you finance the first trip?" I asked.

"Is that any of his business?" demanded Alvin.

"Yes, I think so," responded Josie quietly. "If Mr. Sean is going to help us figure out what's going on, he needs to know everything there is."

"And?" demanded the older Pederson, raising his head and fixing me with a stare. "I'll tell you frankly, I originally thought Josie and Tod's idea to travel all the way to that speck of coral in the Pacific Ocean was a bad idea. Dangerous. But they persisted, and I guess all the research was maybe paying off. Am I right?" He showed his teeth at Tod and Josie. "Although when the day's done, I don't know what you'll have. We already know Amundson died when one of those planes went down, right? Nothing's going to change that. Right?"

"Everybody here and some others contributed," said Tod. "But Josie's dad contributed most of the support." Preston nodded in acknowledgement, and now there was an uncomfortable feel to the air around me. My detective's radar was screeching in my head. I wondered just how eager the old man had been to finance the expeditions.

Maxine bounced up and said, "I'm thirsty. Can't we have some iced tea or something?" It was a tension breaker. Josie stood up and Preston shoved back his chair.

"I'll be right back," he said.

Conversation waned while Josie and Pederson were gone. It still wasn't clear to me why the family had gathered, except I was getting the feeling they were all invested in this enterprise, financially as well as emotionally. It would put a different spin on things.

Chapter 4

With Preston temporarily gone from the gathering, the others seemed to relax, and I wondered about that. My private virtual secretary, the one in my head, was working overtime, taking notes, remembering phrases, making impressions. One of these days I'd buy a small tape recorder.

Josie came back with a tray of tall glasses of iced tea. I noted that Alvin had opted for something that looked suspiciously like a Bloody Mary. Tod took a long drink from his glass and said, "After our first trip to Yap we started to hear from the families of other MIAs, so we organized a group to help collect information and put some of the missing pieces together."

"There are several vets organizations around that function as research and as historical record-keeping groups," Josie said. "Thing is, the war recedes in our collective memories, and government records often don't have the emotional flavor of the events." She paused and her gaze seemed to travel once more into the distant past. "There are a lot of men still missing. I mean, we know they died in the war, but we don't really *know*, if you get my meaning."

I nodded. I understood, even though I had never been to war, or in the service. But I knew people who had gone to Vietnam. Iraq. Even Afghanistan. And not come back. They were killed in action, but their bodies weren't recovered. So families had holes in the fabric of their lives. There were a lot of gaps, a lot of unsaid goodbyes among relatives of the men and women who went to fight in the Pacific during World War II. It would always be that way.

Josie said." I never knew my granduncle, you know? I barely knew my grandfather. But once I started thinking about it, I wanted to know more. So I read a lot and my favorite husband," she smiled and tapped Tod on the shoulder, "encouraged me."

"We joined a group of relatives from Minnesota. There are chapters all over the country, trying to piece records together. We have a website, you know."

"So I understand," I said. I didn't say I hadn't been to it. Surfing the Web was definitely not my thing. I supposed I'd have to ask my neighbors, the Revulon cousins, to do some searching for me.

"Well, we're raising money for more trips to try to find exactly where my relative's plane went down. It was a Liberator, a B-24."

"Tod told me a lot of planes were lost over Yap."

"That's right. U.S. forces bombed the facilities frequently. Because of its location, the Japanese built an important radio and command center there. For a long time the plan was to invade Yap in 1944. But plans changed and allied forces skipped to Leyte and Mindanao in the Philippines.

"When the war ended in forty-five, the garrison on Yap surrendered. It was still in Japanese hands."

"All right, that's the history and that's how your relative, Amundson, came to be shot down there. Let's talk about how I can help you, because I have to tell you, the whole business sounds way outside my areas of expertise." I glanced up to see Preston, Josie's father, returning to settle into the same chair he'd left a few minutes earlier.

"Sorry," he muttered. "Did I miss anything important?"

I opened my mouth and then closed it again. *Important? Yes, you could say that, information important to me, anyway.* I assumed Preston had already heard or read the history of the war itself, and his family involvement.

Tod picked up the narrative. "We think the air raid we're studying was a kind of pickup group. Some of the aircraft appear to have come from a different bomber squadron. Records indicate one plane was loaned to the attacking squadron as a pathfinder. You know what that is?"

As it happened, I did, and I said so. "It's a lone airplane that flies in and marks the target with flares or incendiaries for the bomber group following."

Josie nodded. "That was the plane my granduncle was on. Thing is, he wasn't part of the regular crew. Somebody on Los Negros, we think, arranged to get him aboard the pathfinder which was then to continue after Yap to another destination.

"The pilot radioed that they had successfully located the target. It was at night and there were some storms in the area. Anyway, the last radio transmission from the pilot said they'd turned away after marking the targets and were heading for their planned destination."

"Was that common," I wondered aloud, "using a plane with a different destination, essentially a non-combat mission, to lead a bombing raid?"

"Who knows," Tod said. "What we do know is they did lots of non-regulation things during the war. Expediency. And face it, command and control or whatever they called it then probably wasn't as tight as it should have been."

"So, your granduncle was a non-combatant?"

Josie shook her head. "Oh, he was in combat all right. He flew co-pilot on many missions in the South Pacific. According to what I have found out, he was going to Hawaii to collect a new plane to bring to a forward base, and this was a way to get him to Hawaii. Since he was already ordered to go to Hawaii, somebody asked him to carry a dispatch case for the base commander instead of sending the report on a special flight.

"We know this because he wrote a letter home posted the same day his plane was shot down. In the letter he gripes a little about carrying a dispatch case and a package."

"You have the letter?"

Josie nodded. "My grandmother gave it to me. Anyway, after we started talking to people by phone and letter and by email, it got kind of exciting and we actually went to Yap and dove over some of the known sites where wrecks were located. We planned another trip for later this summer but then things started to happen.

"A smaller but similar group on the East Coast started out very enthusiastic and promised to share some important documents they said they had. But then they disappeared."

"Disappeared. As in vanished?"

"Exactly," Tod said.

"The people in the East Coast group?" I said.

"No, no," Josie jumped in. "Not them, the papers."

"Oh, sorry," Tod said. "Yes, I meant the documents. We got a phone call from someone who said he was the head of the group. I think his name was Charlie something. I've got notes about it somewhere."

"What sort of documents or records are we talking about?" I said.

"Individual service records. Command records of plane disbursements, newspaper and magazine articles. All copies, of course. Most came from the VA or the Department of the Army," Tod said.

"Okay."

Tod took a sip of his drink. "Anyway, he said the documents had gone missing. He sounded upset but he didn't tell me much, except that some records were gone."

"What was in the missing documents?"

"We were told the missing stuff was documentation of a military investigation that happened after the war. Apparently the investigation turned up evidence of smuggling. The papers are supposed to reveal names and places and dates of the illegal activity."

"If they got the report from the government it must have been a copy. The original may still exist somewhere," I said.

Tod shrugged. "I guess so."

"I take it there are links to Yap or the bomber groups that were active there during the war? Is that what this is all about?" I was beginning to feel the waters rising over my head. To say I was swimming out of my depth would be an understatement.

Tod stood up, then he sat again. "No. That isn't it. At least, I don't think so. See, I think the guy with the dispatch case might have been part of a group of GIs sending drugs and maybe other stuff home during the war."

"And the military authorities said what? Did they accuse Amundson?"

"Wait," said Tod. He held up a hand like he was trying to stop the inevitable. "This is getting too fragmented. The documents apparently say the dispatch case or the package the officer was carrying may have contained contraband, but he might not have been aware of it. We think, but we aren't sure, that the man with the dispatch case referred to in some documents was her granduncle."

I stared at Tod and Josie. I got it. "You think some people in the military, because of this investigation, believe your granduncle might have been involved in a smuggling operation, and you want me to look into it? You're thinking there's no way your granduncle could have been involved in something illegal, right? He's under suspicion because he was in the right place at the right time. Circumstances."

"That's right," Josie said. "If there *was* smuggling of any kind, we think if you can find out where the U.S. end of the smuggling was, maybe we'll be able to at least satisfy the family that my granduncle wasn't involved."

"Your family," I said. Josie looked blank. She didn't get it. Tod blinked and sort of flinched. Light flashed in my eyes. Sunlight reflected off the diamond in the pinky ring on Preston's finger. I shifted slightly to the right.

"You know about the Freedom of Information Act?" I asked.

"Sure, we're filing requests all the time. This guy who's coming up here from St. Louis says he has more than the official version of the smuggling investigation. But he refused to tell me anything else until we meet face to face."

"What does he have to say?" I was starting to have trouble keeping all the parts and players in my head. I wished I'd started a notebook when I first arrived.

"His name's Stan Lewis. Stan Lewis from Saint Louis," smiled Tod. "He's arriving tonight by train. He said after he got out of the service he never wanted to fly in anything ever again and he hasn't. He gets in around seven. I'd like you to be there with me to meet him, if you will. He's acted kind of hinky on the phone. He claims people have been asking about him, people he doesn't know. Mr. Lewis said he'd bring some of what he's collected. If he decides everything's jake, he'll turn them over to us."

Cloak and dagger stuff, I mused. "All right, I can do that this evening. What else?"

"What else," said Preston Pederson, "is that we've invested a lot of time and effort and money in this project, and I want to be sure things work out for the best. Now we think somebody's trying to interfere so we won't find the plane that was carrying my dad's brother."

Tod and Josie, with occasional interruptions from Preston, spent another half-hour explaining to me that pieces of gear had gotten vandalized, adding to their expenses, that promises of support funds were reneged. A couple out-of-town individuals who had made plans to join the expedition to Yap that fall abruptly changed their minds. All this was happening without adequate explanations. Suddenly phone calls and emails weren't returned. Letters *were* returned, unopened.

"It's like there's a quiet conspiracy out there to prevent us from making the trip in September." Josie scowled. "I'd hate it if we have to abandon our trip."

"I know, my dear," murmured Preston, "but the money isn't unlimited."

Conspiracy to derail the search was exactly what it sounded like to me, but I wasn't ready to agree with that theory. "All right," I said. "You want me to be at the station when this Stan Lewis arrives this evening, and you want to know why and who, if anybody, is trying to get you to stop this search for your granduncle's plane. And, I presume, you want to know why it's happening.

"Let's leave it there for now. Tod, I'll meet you at the old Union Depot when the train arrives with Stan Lewis. We'll talk to him and then see where we are. Agreed?"

Naturally, everybody agreed, at least they said so, so I departed White Bear. Left unsaid was the implication that learning the "why" of it could turn out to be deeply disrupting. Also left unsaid was the gorilla in the closet. That would be Uncle Amundsen maybe being revealed as a smuggler.

CHAPTER 5

T HE TRAIN FROM CHICAGO carrying Mr. Lewis was sheduled to arrive
at seven. The sun was still pretty far up, daylight saving time and all,
when I drove to the station in downtown Saint Paul. Tod was there
ahead of me. There weren't a lot of people in the cavernous waiting area. This
was my first time into the old station, and I was impressed by the extensive
renovations. Tod and I shook hands and sat down to wait. The train was running late. Something delayed it out of Winona, according to an announcement over the public address system.

The place was surprisingly crowded by the time the train finally slid
into sight. A lot of people apparently wanted to get out of town early that
night. We were prohibited from going onto the platform, so we waited by
the double glass doors. Tod had brought a hand-painted sign that said MR.
LEWIS on it. A tall black man walked up and stood in front of us. It was unnecessary. There was plenty of room. Tod looked distressed.

"Excuse me," I tapped the big guy on his bicep. "You're blocking the
view."

"Yeah?" He looked around, then down at me. I don't know what he
thought he saw in my face, but he shrugged and moved aside. Maybe he just
hadn't seen me at first.

Nineteen people got off the train at St. Paul. I counted them. After
it was clear Mr. Stan Lewis wasn't among those nineteen, I motioned to Tod
and we went to the counter. "Excuse me," I said to the bored-appearing man
who eventually wandered out of the office behind the counter.

"Help you?"

"Do you have any word on why the train was delayed in Winona?"

He looked at me for a long moment. Finally he said, "I don't know
nothin' 'cept the cops are involved. It's a *police matter*."

His emphasis on *police matter* made me wonder. It appeared he didn't care much for me, the day, his job, or law enforcement, for that matter. "Thanks," I said, smiling sweetly. I turned to Tod and we left the terminal. At his car, I suggested he try to reach Mr. Lewis as soon as possible and that I'd drive out to his place in White Bear Lake in the morning.

Tod agreed, saying, "It worries me Lewis didn't show up. He seemed eager to show me the information he's collected over the years."

Late as it was, I went to my office and did some paperwork. One of the bad parts of being a sole proprietor is the routine crap you have to deal with constantly in order to stay on the right side of the law. It was harder to get a PI license than to become a dentist in this state and there was no such thing as malpractice insurance. I drafted answers to a query from my lawyer and wrote a check to my dental insurance company. Nothing dramatic or exciting, just boring routine.

Then I called my friend Ricardo at the Minneapolis cop shop. He had a job like mine, worked odd and fragmented hours, regardless of shift assignments. "I'm curious," I said after the usual greetings.

"Of course you are," he said. "Someday you'll call just to shoot the shit, and I'll be so surprised I'll go into cardiac arrest."

I ignored the remark and said, "I was at the Amtrak station this evening to meet a fella. The train was delayed in Winona because of a police matter."

"And you are interested because . . . ?"

"Because my guy didn't show and because I am nosy."

"Who's your guy?"

"Humor me. I'll tell you later."

Simon sighed into the phone. "Games. I'll get back to you."

I went back to paper shuffling. Fifteen minutes later Ricardo called me. "Here's your unnamed source. We aim to serve. I'm telling or maybe warning you that your inquiry is now part of the official case file."

"Really? Why would that be?"

Ricardo chuckled. "Sean, I suspect you already know the answer. Partly because I called Winona and guess what? The detective in charge was still in his office, late as it is."

"So, enlighten me."

"It's a murder investigation. A man fell off the train at Winona when Amtrak stopped there this afternoon. He died."

"Why is this murder?"

"Bullet hole in the back of the head. Train pulled in, people got on and off, train departed. Body was then discovered. Train was stopped and returned to the station. It hadn't left the city limits, even."

"I bet there'll be some interesting jurisdictional problems, don't you think?"

"I think. I'm also enjoined to ask you a few questions."

"Ask away, but maybe we can short-circuit this if you'll answer a couple first."

"Go." Ricardo and I went back years. I'd always tried to maintain reasonable relationships with cops in the places I was active. Why fight? They had resources I didn't and sometimes I could go places they couldn't without a complicated legal process. A symbiotic relationship, you might call it.

"Old guy?" I began.

"Yes, probably in his late eighties or even early nineties. But he appeared trim and in reasonable shape, according to the detective."

"Any identification?"

"Not the usual, but he had a small World War Two campaign pin on his jacket collar. We don't know yet what campaign. He could have been a vet. Right age. His wallet is missing."

"Where was he coming from? Anything on that?"

"Yes, the train people know he got on in Chicago. He tripped getting into the car from the platform and a porter helped him. That porter didn't know the dead guy's name, but he has the impression the man was traveling from someplace else. Not a Chicagoan. By now of course the Amtrack people will have traced his ticket but if you know anything . . ."

I sighed. "Okay, chief. There's a possibility your dead body was the guy I planned on meeting tonight. If so, his name is Stan Lewis." I spelled it. "And he's from St. Louis. He's a veteran all right. The campaign button is from World War Two, the South Pacific Theater. I never met the guy so I can't give you a description, but I can maybe get you an address or a phone number if you give me until morning."

"Excellent," said Ricardo. "I'll pass this along to Winona and wait for your call."

We hung up and I went home to bed.

* * * *

FIRST THING IN THE MORNING, I called Bartelmes. There was no answer. On a hunch I looked up Pres Pederson in the phone book. There still are such things, although the proliferation of telephone services makes any one of the several available books no longer complete. Then you have all these cell phones with no book at all. But Pederson had a business and an office and a listing. He was in.

"Mr. Pederson, this is Sean Sean, the detective."

"Yes. How can I help you?" He sounded a lot more polite in his business persona.

"I'm trying to reach either your son-in-law or daughter. It's a matter of some urgency. They didn't answer at home."

"I think they've both gone to the storage facility in Maplewood. Something about a possible break-in last night."

"Damn! Do you have that address?" He did and read it to me. I dropped the phone and left the office, headed for Maplewood.

Half an hour later I stood amongst cops and storage company workers in front of a large compartment in one of those ubiquitous facilities you see from almost every highway. We seem to be accumulating more and more stuff we won't discard, and sharp entrepreneurs have appeared to provide storage for our belongings. Personally, if there's no room for it in my house, there's no room for it in my life. So I have traded, sold or given away a lot of things for which I have had no further use. So far, no regrets, either.

Josie and Tod were there. I had talked my way through the tall chain link and barbed wire security fence by verbally dancing with the guy in the office, and found them looking with joint consternation into the large compartment. It was filled almost to overflowing. There was a lot of furniture, some of it overturned, an old-fashioned bureau, its drawers pulled out and two upturned on the floor. A cracked mirror lay on its side. Bent picture frames in an untidy stack spilled onto the floor beside the overhead door.

"What do we have?" I asked.

"It looks like theft and vandalism," said Josie, a tremor in her voice.

"What's missing?"

"We haven't checked thoroughly 'cause we're waiting for more police. Detectives, I guess. But I can see all our diving gear is gone. It's all replaceable, of course, but it represents a lot of money." Tod sighed and scratched his arm. Then he looked down. "I've got to get this rash cleared up or I won't be able to dive even if we get to the island this fall."

"Any other units broken into?"

Josie looked at me and shook her head. "No. So this is probably another incident designed to keep us from going back to the South Pacific."

"Both a warning and a delay."

Tod grimaced. "Somebody doesn't want us to go back to Yap."

"I think that's it exactly," I said. "The question is why. If we knew that, we'd probably know who. Do you know when this break-in happened?"

"The storage people called us early this morning. I guess somebody drives around the place every so often. Daily. They noticed the lock on the overhead door was damaged."

"When was the last time you were here?"

Josie wrinkled her brow and said, "A week ago, I think. There's no reason to come until we need the diving gear."

"Could the person who did this have been looking for records? Where do you keep the research you've been doing? All the stuff people are sending you?"

Tod started to tell me when the Maplewood squad car showed up behind us, and the Bartelmes had to go through an extensive interview.

Half an hour later the cops departed with all their forms properly filled in. Tod watched them go. "They don't seem hopeful."

"Non-violent burglaries are not a high priority. I'm surprised they didn't let the uniforms handle it. Let's go back to the questions I asked when the cops showed up."

"We keep all the records in a climate-controlled room here. It's a separate building." He waved toward a squat concrete block building at the end of the aisle. "The room we have there hasn't been touched. Do you think they were looking for the files?"

In answer, I said, "I called around to find out why the train was delayed in Winona. There was a death. An old man was found beside the platform after the train pulled out, so the train was stopped." I positioned myself so I could watch their faces. I wasn't a hundred percent sure yet that my clients were clean in this affair.

"That's terrible," said Josie.

Tod stared at me. "You said an old man. Could that have been . . . ?" His voice trailed off.

I nodded. "The man was the right age but he didn't have any identification on him. And there's one other thing." There was no easy way to say this. "He was murdered." Josie's face went white, and her mouth opened and closed. Tod swayed and reached out to clutch his wife's arm.

"My God," he whispered. "It must be Mr. Lewis. Is that possible?"

"I think it's likely. Anything else would be too coincidental. I gave the police that lead and they'll run it down. If you have an address or a telephone number for Lewis, we should get it to the Winona Police right away.

"There's another thing," I continued. "If this is the right person, he was traveling very light. According to my source, they haven't found a wallet, an overnight bag or a suitcase, and there are no papers."

Tod stared at me. "So?"

"If it is your Stan Lewis, and he was bringing you some old World War Two records, they're gone."

Josie looked at Tod and her face crumpled. I could see Tod slumping slightly. This information was a real blow to them. I concluded my clients were not perpetrators of these crimes. I handed Tod a piece of paper with the number for the Winona police department. "You need to call them with anything you can tell them about Lewis. I've asked a friend to let me know as soon as the identification is made." I was satisfied. If Tod or Josie had prior knowledge of the murder of the man in Winona, their acting was remarkable.

Chapter 6

BEFORE I LEFT THE BARTELMES, I learned they weren't sure how much information Stan Lewis from St. Louis had been bringing to Minnesota. He'd remained suspicious enough I thought it worth a shot to get in touch with the St. Louis police to suggest they check out the old man's residence.

I did this through Ricardo. I knew a call from some unknown PI in Minnesota wouldn't get much attention, especially since the murder of the as-yet-unidentified old man off the train had happened a long way from their jurisdiction.

Only an hour later, around noon, Ricardo called back to tell me he talked to a detective in St. Louis, who did a search of 911 calls and learned there had been an apparent burglary at an apartment in the city. The address was listed to a Stanley Lewis. When the cops broke down the door, his place had been thoroughly trashed. It appeared, Ricardo related, that the break-in had happened about the time Stan was arriving in Chicago. The St. Louis cops had put the burglary down to somebody looking for drugs or fenceable items. It was impossible to tell, without the owner's help, whether anything was missing.

I called the Bartelmes with the news. "Here's what I think," I said to Tod. "Since there was no wallet and no papers found with the body, you need to reach out right away to your contacts in the vets group to find out anything you can about Stan and what documents he may have had. Maybe it's already too late and the papers are gone from his apartment, but everything you've told me about him so far suggests he may have had a more secure storage place, like a safe deposit box in a bank. That poses problems in itself, but not insurmountable ones. Meanwhile, you may be able to locate a source of copies of whatever Mr. Lewis was bringing you."

"Got it. I'll get on our email list right away and see what I can learn."

"Try to be discreet. The rest of your group doesn't need to know Lewis was murdered. At least, not just yet. And one other thing, Tod."

"What's that?"

"You need to consider that you and Josie are now targets."

"What?"

"If Stan Lewis was murdered for the papers he was carrying, whoever did this may figure you and your wife also have information dangerous to them. You and Josie ought to review everything you can think of that relates to your contacts with Mr. Lewis. Try to recall what he knew about you two and what you've told others. And try not to go anywhere alone. I don't want to frighten you—"

"You're certainly starting to," Tod said.

"Well, I'm sorry, but just be careful and keep track of any odd or unusual contacts. Something's going on here, and it's going to take me some time to figure it out."

I hung up the phone. I didn't tell Tod to stay out of dark alleys. I figured that wasn't anywhere in his experience or future. I went to my file of out-of-town investigators. Many private operators developed professional contacts across the country. I used mine, sometimes paying a fee, other times returning local service where called for. My rolodex revealed I had a years-old contact with a St. Louis area code. I called the number, but it was not in service. I tried Ricardo Simon to see if he knew anybody there. He wasn't in. So then I dialed a local investigator to whom I usually referred divorce cases.

The guy I wanted was in and he had an active contact in St. Louis. With that reference, I called Carl Wisnewsky. He was also in and knew my original contact who, he informed me, had died in bed of nothing more suspicious than natural causes. He agreed for a reasonable fee to look into the Stan Lewis burglary case. I added Carl to my rolodex.

I explained that by now the cops in St. Louis would have heard from Winona and elevated the case to something more than simple burglary. There was no heavy lifting here. I only wanted whatever the cops would let go. He rang off, and I went to my computer to make notes on what I had so far.

Even with my rudimentary understanding of computer systems and the Internet, I was slowly becoming more dependent on the machine for keeping track of case notes and my business. Two things worried me: loss of notes in the mysterious ether of cyberspace, through my ineptitude or a breakdown of the silicon inside the machine, or loss by some thug stealing the machine or its memory. I protected myself against theft by making copies of my notes on those plastic discs called CDs. I taught myself how to use that recording program. Those copies I kept in various secret places, just as I had with paper records. I couldn't do anything about machine problems and I still flinched every time the lights in my office building flickered due to some sudden surge or drain on the electrical system.

Now, as I organized my memories of the people and events of this case of Yap, questions came flooding in. This was a not-uncommon circumstance early on. I didn't yet know all the players well enough to decide whether they were Godless or on the side of the angels.

The telephone rang. Enter Gary Anderson. He was calling, he said, from his office in downtown Minneapolis. It was, I knew, on the umpty-umpth floor of one of the newer towers growing up like spring weeds around the metropolitan core. I could remember as a child in Minnesota, the tallest building in the city was the Foshay Tower, and in St. Paul, the First National Bank building. Now there were towers taller and more spectacular all over the place, although St. Paul seemed determined to avoid overshadowing the big red number one on top of the bank building.

"We were unable to talk privately at the Bartelmes the other day," he said. "A good deal's happened since and I wonder if I might impose on you to meet me today."

"Sure," I said. "I could come to your office in about an hour or so."

"Hmm. I wonder if we could meet for lunch? There's a nice quiet little place near here. Say, eleven-thirty?" He mentioned a name.

"That's fine. I know the place."

Interesting, I thought as I replaced the hand set in its cradle. *He wants to meet but maybe he doesn't want to be seen with me at his office.* Lawyer Anderson was known for his discretion. He was also known in some legal gossip circles as someone who skated close to the edge of the ethical cliff from time to time. His primary focus was manipulation of financial assets for the benefit of his well-off clients and for himself, naturally.

The restaurant, on a short side street in the middle of downtown, had no connection to the skyway system. It was not a place where the up-and-coming young hustlers in the financial or other commercial trades in the city went to see and be seen. This was a small, quiet restaurant with an excellent chef and a highly discreet waitstaff. An awning over the sidewalk sheltered the single street door, but the awning was plain and there was no elaborate lettering on the front window. No lettering on the window at all. The lettering on the door simply gave the street number, which was repeated on the matte black letter-box slot in the wall beside the door.

Inside, the hostess, a well-set-up woman of middling years with a calm demeanor, eyed me as I stepped through the door.

"Good afternoon, sir," she said. Then she waited, looking down at me.

She didn't ask if she could help or be of service. These were not on her agenda.

"I'm meeting Mr. Gary Anderson," I said. "Perhaps he called?"

"Right this way, sir."

She wheeled smartly about, her shoulder-length, straight, ash-blonde hair swinging aside, and led me around the panel that blocked my view of the interior. I had to stretch to keep pace, my legs being shorter than hers. I didn't want to trot, did I?

We passed eight tables, four on the left and four on the right. The blonde hostess stopped at a ninth at the very back, not too far from a door that led, I presumed, to the kitchen and probably certain sanitary facilities as well. Each table, I noted in passing, was laid with a white cloth, cloth napkins, silverware, and wine and water glasses.

I took the chair she pulled for me, so I sat with my back to the room. She left my side and a waiter materialized with a pitcher of water, which he generously shared with me. He also inquired if I wanted a drink. I declined, refraining from requesting a bottle of Bud, just to see what his reaction would be.

The tall, stork-like Gary Anderson, his eyes alight with mischief and with his large hand already extended, walked around the table, waving me down and sank into the chair opposite.

"No trouble finding it, I see," he said. The waiter repeated his routine, and Anderson ordered a dry martini with a twist. "Not drinking this noon?"

"I usually wait until later in the day unless the job calls for it," I said. "And my recollection is that the drinks here are substantial."

Anderson raised his eyebrows. I imagine he was wondering if I was a regular or how frequently I had been here. He had no way of knowing, of course, except that he'd never seen me here. I was not going to enlighten him. I assumed we were engaged in some sort of game to either impress me or frighten me into getting lost, or perhaps into proving my mettle.

I knew a good deal about Mr. Gary Anderson, attorney at law. I had clients, regular clients, who could buy and sell him several times over. That I preferred to hang about with middle- and other-class folks didn't mean I couldn't and didn't make my occasional way in more rarefied circles. I even knew how to find Deephaven, should I ever need to do so.

"I appreciate the lunch invitation, Mr. Anderson. How may I be of service?" Unlike the hostess, whom I could hear behind me seating other guests, I was anxious to get down to the meat of the matter. I figured if I kept a light pressure on, Mr. Attorney Anderson might not only reveal his agenda, but a few other choice tidbits as well. I'm always willing to receive choice tidbits.

He smiled, nodded at someone I couldn't see, and said, "Let's order, shall we? I understand the broiled salmon is quite good today." Then he proceeded to do exactly that, having downed half his martini. For both of us. He didn't order the broiled salmon. Instead we had cold smoked salmon steaks with a small boiled potato and a crisp arugula salad combined with a light balsamic and oil dressing and half a thinly sliced tomato. It was a dynamite lunch and I said so. He airily waved the compliment away. I got the impression he might not have known the difference if the salad was limp iceberg and the salmon was hard and dry, which it certainly wasn't.

He had another dry martini, and I had another glass of water. He took a sip and got down to business, speaking just loudly enough so I could hear him over the other conversations in the room.

CHAPTER 7

As I'm sure you are aware, Mr. . . . . Sean, I have had the privilege of serving the Pederson financial interests for some time, and more recently those of Tod and Josie Bartelme," Gary began. "Even though neither of the Bartelmes has the kind of investment resources our firm normally deals with, we are happy to be assisting Mr. Pederson's daughter to realize a comfortable retirement."

"I assume there's some depletion of those resources going on at the moment."

"Indeed, you assume correctly. This near obsession of Josie's to locate her clearly deceased granduncle Amundson is not only taking up a considerable amount of time, it's now eating into the family retirement resources."

"You needn't go into the details, but I am curious as to why you are telling me this," I said, taking another sip of water.

"I decided it would be wise for you to be in the picture, so to speak, in order for you to better understand current family dynamics. Ordinarily an outsider like yourself wouldn't have this kind of access. I'm aware that Tod and Josie have already talked rather freely, which is their right, of course."

Yeah, their right, and Anderson didn't approve. I could tell.

"Mr. Pederson, out of his not inconsiderable resources, largely financed the first two expeditions to the South Pacific," he continued. "After Tod established the website and they made contact with veterans groups around the nation, and word of their quest got out, some contributions came in. They got a lot more requests for information than they did money, unfortunately. A few people even asked if they could hitchhike along. It is hard to imagine why there seems to be so much interest in this project. There are others, of course. Relatives and historical groups are always looking for missing pieces and as I'm sure you're aware, there are still a considerable number of unrecovered remains from that war."

I agreed he was correct and had some more water. Anderson's empty martini glass had been replaced with a full one. The alcohol he was imbibing had no discernable effect on his speech, and he still leaned confidentially over the table at me. His hands and arms made no histrionic gestures. All in all, it was a pretty good performance.

"Well, as you can understand, after the first two trips, which inevitably cost more than budgeted and resulted in little significant additional information, some of those investing time and money assumed that would be the end of it." He grimaced. "We misjudged the depth of Josie's interest and her husband's support. They both became a bit obsessive. When her father expressed reluctance to finance further trips, they directed me to begin to sell off their investments in order to pay for the trip this fall. Neither her father nor their advisors were pleased with the idea. Nor was the rest of the family, most of whom take a certain proprietary interest in the family fortunes.

"The situation's getting out of hand. Frankly, Mr. . . . Sean, you're an added expense no one expected. Now we have an apparent murder." He spread his hands.

"I take it you'd like me to butt out," I said coarsely. I wondered what his source for the death of Stan Lewis was, but I didn't ask.

"Correct. It appears to us the law enforcement people are capable of handling these recent and most distressing developments. I'm prepared to pay you for your time and expenses up to now, plus a generous bonus. All you have to do is reject Tod's request."

"What do you suggest I tell him?"

Anderson shrugged. "I don't care. Tell him you have a conflict. Tell him your workload is too heavy. Suggest he wants help you don't know how to provide. It really doesn't matter."

Actually, it would matter, if I cared about my business. So, after a nice lunch and some sweet water, I was being offered my walking papers. I told Mr. Anderson I'd think about his suggestion, and I wouldn't charge anything for the time I spent thinking, nor for the time we spent at lunch. I also mentioned he could expect to hear from me by the end of the day, barring unforeseen circumstances.

"Thank you, Mr. . . . Sean. I was sure you'd be reasonable in this matter. Please call me at this number with your decision." He slid a business card across the white tablecloth to me. It had a number printed on it by hand. I saw right away it was not his office number. *So,* I thought. *He wants to keep things as far away from his regular business as possible. Perhaps he doesn't want his partners and associates to know about this at all. Now why would that be?*

DeLoite, Anderson, Martin, and Norton was a well-known and respected firm. No serious scandal had ever attached itself to them, although they had a reputation for aggressive courtroom tactics and preferred financial clients who lined up on the riskier side of the investment equation. So what was this attempt to separate me from the Bartelme affair all about?

That was a question for another time. I took the card, rose from my chair and nodded to Mr. Anderson. He didn't respond as I turned and walked back toward the front of the restaurant. It was noteworthy that, like my previous visits, no one at the other tables even glanced my way. I knew telephones and small office cabals would remark that day that lawyer Gary Anderson had been seen at lunch with a small man almost no one could identify by name. I was sure most of those who did know me by name would not be eager to reveal it.

As a private investigator, private was my stock in trade. It was what I emphasized. I avoided getting my name in the papers. Building a reputation as discreet and anonymous was important to what I did. And I was good at what I did. When I cracked a case, even a big case, sometimes involving prominent people, they often got their names in the news. Not me. So I would remain a mystery to most of those whom I passed in that restaurant. Good deal.

* * * *

I'D TOLD ANDERSON I'd think about his offer. His slimy offer. I wasn't going to accept it, but I sat at my desk and considered it, because there might be clues there to what was going on in this case. I still couldn't figure out why anyone would care about an obscure attempt by ordinary Minnesotans to locate the grave of a relative killed in the Pacific Ocean. Now I had a lawyer, part of the family support system, presumably, trying to buy me off. One of the other pins on which a PI rested his professional life was his perceived integrity. I liked mine, and I was going to keep it.

The murder of veteran Stan Lewis while he was presumably bringing information to the Bartelmes was more than a little worrisome as well. These two recent events combined with the sabotage that was on the rise said somebody was upset about Tod and Josie's search efforts. I was going to have to talk with them again about abandoning their quest altogether or at least persuade them to employ a little personal security. It would not be a fun talk and I knew it had to be face to face.

I called the Bartelme residence and learned they'd both be available that evening. I'd barely hung up the phone when my man in Saint Louis was on the horn.

"It's definite a search of Lewis's apartment was made about the time he was on the train to Saint Paul," my contact told me. "The police are also sure the place was ripped up to conceal a thorough search for something."

"How thorough was the search?"

"Interesting you should ask that. Very. For example, grates on the heating ducts were pulled off. The searchers replaced the duct covers, but it was obvious they'd all been removed. Tracks in the dust confirmed it. The other thing is that usually you can tell when a search stops. The searchers just quit, and there are signs where they stopped. Not in this case."

"Which means we can be confident they didn't find what they were looking for or they wanted to conceal that the break-in was for a purpose other than finding saleable stuff."

"Exactly. These were not your ordinary street-level, smash-and-grab boys. They were smart, thorough and careful. I don't know what you have going up there in Minnesota, and I'm not sure I want to know."

"I get your point," I said. "We seem to be bumping up against a fairly sophisticated operation. Thanks for your help. Send me a bill."

We concluded our connection and I went home, thinking hard. There appeared to be considerably more layers to this case.

Chapter 8

That evening I decided I needed to know a good deal more about Yap Island and its place in the grand scheme of things back in the forties. So I went to the library and then I went to the Internet to do some research.

The next morning I called my good friend and main squeeze, Catherine Mckerney.

"Say, fella," she said, "I'm missing you a good deal here. What's going on?"

"A case, of course. One filled with murky details, sexy broads, pricey jewels, gold bars, murder, mayhem, and the usual list of questions with few or misleading answers. I spent last evening at the library and I think I may be more confused than when I started."

"Sounds to me like we should have an evening in and discuss things," she said, putting into words what I realized I was subconsciously hoping to hear. I sometimes discussed elements of my cases, when Catherine was willing. Gave me a different perspective, and sometimes good answers.

"That'd be fabulous," I purred. "I'll arrive in time to mix a pitcher of Sangria. Or maybe some exotic kind of hot-climate libation."

She chuckled in my ear. "I love it when you talk dirty to me. See you later, lover."

But it was not to be. Not that evening. There was a shooting that afternoon. I got the call from a frantic Tod Bartelme.

"Can you come right away? Calvin's in the hospital. He's been shot." Tod let out a single large sob and struggled to go on. "We're at St. John's East. Know where that is?"

Regrettably, I did. I had made it my business to know the best routes to every hospital in the area. I got in my car and tore east, bypassing a couple of lakes in my way, and made it to the hospital in record time. No police squads hampered my run. In the Intensive Care section of the relatively new facility, I found both Josie and Tod in a state of shock, restlessly waiting for news from the doctors who were somewhere behind the swinging doors to the operating suites. They paced across the small waiting alcove.

Josie looked terrible. Her eyes were puffy, and tears left silvery tracks on her pale cheeks. She was casually dressed in a loose t-shirt and jeans. She wore her brown topsiders without socks. Her hands trembled, and the wad of tissue she held was quickly succumbing to the picking of her restless fingers.

Tod had obviously rushed to the hospital from work. His conservative suit was rumpled, and he'd yanked his tie down and opened the collar of his shirt. He kept running his fingers through his already messy brown hair.

"Tell me what happened," I demanded. "Everything you can remember. Have the cops been notified?"

Josie gulped, wiped her nose and took a deep breath to try to calm herself. We stared at each other. "I was home. Calvin and some of the neighborhood kids were swimming and fooling around on the beach. Our beach."

"We collaborated with the neighbors on either side to make kind of a swimming area with a small diving platform," Tod muttered.

"It's a float. We anchor it about twenty feet off the beach so the water's deep enough for diving. The diving board's only six feet off the water," Josie said. She waved one hand and dropped a tissue. "Anyway, they were taking turns cannonballing off the board, you know?"

I nodded. I knew what that was. Cannonballing, a common lake activity, especially for young and vital teens, had you run off the board, tuck knees and arms and make a great splash, usually near some friends. If you did it right, the wave was big, and the water stung your back just a little when you hit it. Whooping and hollering were usually part of the act.

"So when Calvin went up and jumped off, he hit the water sort of funny, more stretched out," Josie said. "That's what Jeff told us. Jeff Brooks. He's the next-door neighbor. Nice kid. Anyway, Jeff said Calvin surfaced but he didn't roll over or swim or anything. First they thought he was faking it. Calvin was drowning." She swallowed some air and Tod put his arm around

41

her again, turning her face into his shoulder. Josie let him hold her for a moment then she pushed away. "One of the boys grabbed Calvin and rolled him over. He wasn't breathing." Josie began to sob then, leaning over at the waist. Her knees bent as if she couldn't stand any longer.

Tod put his hands on her shoulders again and eased her back onto the sofa. He sank down beside her and ran one arm across her shoulders, squeezing gently. He took a deep breath and continued the story, "We don't know how close to death he came. Too damn close, anyway. When they pulled him ashore and started CPR, one of the boys noticed blood on his shoulder, and there was a hole in the skin." He shook his head. "Apparently nobody heard a shot. What kind of fool shoots off a gun in a place like that? It's insane."

None of us noticed the silent approach of a doctor in rumpled pale blue surgicals with yellow booties until she was right next to us. I didn't see any blood on her scrubs. She pulled her mask down and said. "You're the Bartelmes?"

Tod acknowledged they were. There was a minute pause as if we were all afraid to continue. Finally, Tod stood and said. "How's Calvin? Is he all right?"

"He's fine, and he should fully recover, physically." The doctor nodded. "A small-caliber bullet penetrated his shoulder and exited just above the scapula, the big bone that makes the wing on the back. He's very lucky. The bullet missed major arteries and did very little damage to the muscles in his shoulder and back. With proper therapy, he'll be fine. There's no bone damage at all."

I looked at the doctor. She glanced at me and then in a lower voice said, "I recommend Calvin have some counseling after he recovers some. Being shot, even with minimal damage, can be very traumatic."

"You've notified the police, I assume," I said.

"Of course. They'll be here any time now for your statement. It's required with all gunshot wounds, even accidental ones." The physician looked at Josie and then back at me. I could see she was wondering about my role in this.

"Can we see him?" asked Josie.

"Of course. He's not yet out of the anesthetic, but he'll wake up in a little while. You can sit with him." The doctor turned to lead the Bartelmes to recovery.

I took Tod's arm, and we lagged a step behind. "You aren't sure this was an accident, are you," I murmured.

He turned his head and said in a low voice, "That's why I called you. With everything that's happened, I just want the rest of us to be safe."

I nodded. "I'll check it out. But I better not stay. Is the house open?"

"Yes. Somebody is there pretty much all the time." He turned to go and I heard an undertone in his voice that suggested he wasn't entirely happy with some of his guests.

I slowed and let them get a step or two ahead. "I'll be in touch, Mr. Bartelme." The doctor's head came up. She was going to mention me to the cops. Josie didn't look back. The trio disappeared down the wide hall and through a door to the recovery wing. Across the room an elevator dinged and two uniformed officers appeared. I nodded at them and headed for the stairs. In the ground floor lobby I found two quarters in my pocket and went to the bank of phones hanging on one wall. It was a small bank. The proliferation of cell phones has reduced the need for public pay phones in hospitals and other buildings by quite a bit.

I left a quick message for Catherine that I was delayed and not to wait dinner. I also mentioned I was looking forward to some pillow talk a little later. Then I beat it out of there. I needed to get to Bartelmes' without delay. In the car I made a couple of quick notes on my conversation with Tod and Josie and drove to their home. When I pulled up and parked, the neighborhood seemed unnaturally quiet. The air was still and hot. The last time I was in that driveway I recalled I'd been able to hear the sounds of suburbia: a distant mower, kids, birds, and dogs. Now it seemed as if there was a collective pause, a silence while the neighborhood waited to learn Calvin's fate. Maybe it was just me.

"He's going to be fine," I said. Then I said it a little louder, maybe to persuade myself, maybe I was trying to reassure the fence, or the garage, or the birds in the bushes. I wasn't sure, but I said it again, firmly, out loud. A tiny breeze stirred the lilac bush beside the fence where Calvin had met me. I pushed through the gate and walked around the house to find three people on the deck clutching tall drinks. They looked like rum. The drinks did.

Alvin Pederson was closest, standing beside a small mobile bar loaded with the makings of various cocktails. He was about to add ice to a depleted drink when I appeared.

Farther along, sprawled primly in a chaise was his wife, Maxine. Her glass was empty except for what appeared to be a dark straw. She smiled and did one of those things with her shoulders that women know how to do. It made her thin blue blouse gap wider in front. She didn't appear to be wearing a bra. When she smiled up at me as I advanced up the steps, I deduced that she'd been drinking. Her look had that almost-focused gaze of too much booze too fast or on an empty stomach.

The third porch squatter was a man I had barely met at the last rendezvous, Richard Hillier. Although we weren't personally acquainted, I knew a few things about him. He had been associated with Preston Pederson for many years. From what I'd gathered so far, he was an untitled bag man, an associate unafraid to get his hands dirty should that be necessary. He was big, maybe two hundred fifty pounds on a wide, heavy-boned frame. In his day, he would have been a fearsome adversary. But his day was gone on the wings of time, too much drink, rich fatty foods, and not enough exercise. Even so, he could probably wipe the floor with me. If he could catch me.

He turned his face toward me silently and then, with a certain deliberation, raised his glass to his lips. He wore a pair of dark aviator-style sunglasses that effectively concealed his eyes. Cool, very cool.

"Tod and Josie aren't here," Pederson said, adding an ice cube to his glass. He didn't bother to use tongs.

"I know," I said. "I just came from the hospital."

CHAPTER 9

HILLIER RAISED ONE EYEBROW and looked at me. "So you know about Calvin being shot."

"I'm here to check out the circumstances." I paused by Mrs. Pederson's chaise and ogled her bosom for a second.

"What's the point of that?" whined her husband. "What can you do about some neighbor nutcase firing off a gun?"

I didn't make the obvious response that there were some unanswered questions, such as where, who, and why. More than just some, actually. "Detecting is what I do," I said. I thought I was being satisfactorily obscure. I allowed my mouth to curve slightly in a somewhat enigmatic smile. I thought it was, anyway.

"If you need a guide around the place, I'll be happy to oblige," said Maxine. She put out her hand for help rising from the couch. Since I was closest, it seemed only polite I offer her my hand.

"Oh, for Chrissake, Max! Give it a break. You come on to every upright male that shows up with a half a wit." I turned my gaze on him. Alvin's face took on a decidedly unhealthy color. He gulped down half his drink. For his gut's sake, I hoped it wasn't too strong.

"I appreciate the offer, Mrs. Pederson." I said, mostly to bug Alvin. "You can show me the way to the second-floor rooms that look out on the lake." I didn't use my Bogart imitation.

"Oh, you want to see the bedrooms?" Her grin was predatory. Her husband shuddered, and Hillier seemed to stare impassively. Maxine missed their reactions as she spun on her heels and led me through the sliding patio door. Once out of sight of the two men on the patio, her attitude de-escalated and she stalked ahead of me to the stairs that led, I learned, first to a landing, then to the long second-floor hall that bisected the house. There were five rooms on the second floor, Maxine told me, four being used as bedrooms, but only two faced the lake. One was the master bedroom with a broad sliding glass wall that led to a narrow balcony directly over the patio. I could hear Pederson and Hillier in conversation. From her stance, I figured Maxine was straining to hear what they were saying.

The other bedroom had no balcony, was smaller, comfortable with a queen-sized bed and a highly polished armoire instead of a closet. The windows did look out on the lake. By twisting my head I could get a narrow look through the removable screen at the swim area, but it was an awkward position at best.

Maxine turned arch as we went back to the hall. "My room is over there," she said, gesturing across my chest.

"Since you have no view of the lake, I won't need to see it," I said. "I take it you and your husband live here with the Bartelmes?"

Her hesitation was miniscule, but I caught it. "Oh, no, but we're here for Josie and Tod during these troubles. You know." Her voice trailed off as if she wasn't sure how to respond. What was that all about? I filed her reaction in my mental tickler file, and we went back downstairs.

I had the names and addresses of two of the boys who had been at the Bartelmes' beach when Calvin was injured. They were on a crumpled scrap of paper Josie had thrust at me at the hospital. I hoped to get an eyewitness account of the shooting. I walked down to the edge of the lake, alone. Maxine had declined to accompany me into the hot sun. I looked at the empty floating raft with its low diving platform. It was altogether a peaceful summer scene. I found it hard to believe what had happened.

Voices arose on my left from the adjoining property. A hedge separated the properties, but no fence. The location was one of the two I had for boys on the scene earlier that afternoon, so I pushed through the hedge and found myself on another beach with a short dock in the middle of the property.

Three boys about Calvin's age sprawled on the beach in their swimsuits. A fourth thrashed through the water toward the beach, making a great laughing, sputtering production out of it. The other three were flicking sand and water droplets at each other. When I appeared, fully dressed, a stranger, they turned immediately serious. I walked forward holding their attention while the fourth boy struggled toward us out of the lake.

"My name's Sean Sean," I said. "I'm working for Tod and Josie Bartelme."

"You're the PI," one of them said, "with the same first and last names. Cool."

"How's Cal doing?" another asked.

"He's going to be fine," I said. There was immediate reduction in the tension. The boys relaxed. "Now I need some help. Which one of you answers to the name of Jeff Brooks?"

Teenager automatic distrust of adults asserted itself. The boys glanced at each other, not saying anything. Except two of them looked at the same boy.

"This is no big deal. I just want to try to recreate the shooting. I know you and some of your friends were on Bartelmes' beach when it went down." I stared at Jeff Brooks. "You were the closest, according to what I've been told. I suppose these other fellows were there too, right? Now, the cops are gonna be here soon to get formal statements. Your parents are probably being notified and lawyers rounded up. There'll be delays while routines are followed. I just want to find out what happened to your friend, whatever you saw, as near as possible before things get complicated."

I spread my hands and looked at them. The boy I'd figured was Jeff stood up. "I'm Jeff Brooks," he said. We shook hands.

"Let's go next door," I said, and we all trooped back through the hedge of lilacs. It turned out my instinct was right, all the boys were there when Calvin got shot. The one who they all agreed had been farthest from the action, Ted something, insisted he didn't actually see anything, so I selected him to be Calvin for my deal. I had my new digital camera with me. The plan was to get a series of pictures of a body flying through the air in the same position as Calvin was. At first it didn't work. For some reason Ted Something-or-other couldn't get his arms and legs in the right position. The boys were serious and pointed out problems in jump after jump.

Finally the Brooks boy came out of the water saying, "Let me try it. I showed Calvin how I do a cannonball. It's with a half twist, like this."

He swam to the dock and did his cannonball with a twist. The other watching boys all enthusiastically agreed that was exactly how Calvin was positioned when he was shot. So I had him do it six more times and took lots of pictures. We all figured he got his arms and legs just right at least four times. That was easier than trying to calculate how high off the water Calvin had been when he was plugged.

It wasn't perfect but I was happy. I thought I'd be able to get pretty close to the place the shooter had stood or laid to make his shot.

When I dismissed the boys with thanks and turned back to the house, I discovered an interested audience. Hillier and Al Pederson were standing, drinks in hand, watching from the lakeside veranda.

"What are you doing?" Pederson inquired.

Normally I wouldn't say. Normally I wouldn't give somebody like Alvin Pederson the time of day. I knew his type. He thought he was an insider and any bits of gossip he could scrape up gave him a supposed advantage over someone. Alvin Pederson was a bottom feeder.

The other reason I wouldn't normally give him a passing glance was that we detectives liked to be a little mysterious from time to time. Other times we weren't sure ourselves what we were doing or why; it's just something that feels right at the time. In this case, I figured it wouldn't hurt to explain and the telling might shake something loose, depending on who they talked to.

"I want to recreate the scene of the crime," I said. "When I look at blowups of these pictures together with pictures of Calvin's injuries, I'll learn a few things."

Both Hillier and Pederson nodded as if they understood exactly what I was saying. I wondered if *I* did as I left the premises and drove back to Roseville.

At home in my basement office I downloaded the digital pictures to my computer and made a series of quick prints on plain paper. I laid out the ones that showed Jeff Brooks in the closest position to Calvin's body when he'd been shot. By superimposing a tracing of the wounds I made from memory, I was able to determine several things. Some of them I already knew.

The shot had been fired from outside the house. I thought it likely the cops would have a tough time recovering the slug. If my calculations were correct, after it passed through Calvin's hand and along his ribs to exit at the top of his shoulder, it had probably tumbled to the ground somewhere in the vicinity of the bramble patch beside the lilacs that separated the Brooks's place from the Bartelmes'.

I pulled a topographic map of that end of the lake from my file. Coincidence? Nah. Over the years I made it my business to collect such documents and even tried to keep them reasonably up to date. Useful tools of the trade.

After some peering and jockeying of the map and a crude drawing I produced for myself, I was able to diagram an oval on the opposite shore of the bay that would have likely been where the shooter had stood. It was far from ideal, but it was a woodsy grove with thick underbrush below the pines and ash trees, so it did provide concealment for the presumed shooter. And the bay was pretty narrow at that point.

I called the hospital to check on Calvin's progress. I got the runaround jabber about patient privacy and they couldn't find either Tod or Josie. I left the house and journeyed back to White Bear along now crowded Highway 96. The afternoon had waned and home-bound traffic was jamming up the road, so it took me longer than usual to get to the place on the other side of the bay where I thought the shooter must have been located.

I pulled the car off onto the shoulder as far as the trees allowed. The left rear fender hung over the white stripe they paint at the outside edge of these roads, but I figured my car was pretty easily seen. I brought my small, efficient pair of binocs along. I walked to the edge of the property and stood on a large boulder and scanned the opposite side of the bay until I located the Brooks place and next to it, the raft and the Bartelme home. The shoreline was empty of people. The sun was still hot and low to the horizon. Behind me critters rustled and muttered in the grass and weeds. A lethargic sparrow hopped from tree branch to tree branch, keeping one eye on me and the other, presumably, alert for any edible tidbit that might turn up.

I walked slowly into the copse. A bramble immediately attacked my left pant leg. I pulled free and scanned the ground around me. It appeared to be an ordinary piece of ground with few tracks, certainly nothing that would indicate the presence of a large two-legged predator. It took several sweaty minutes with no relieving breeze to cover the patch of ground where I figured the shooter must have been. I found nothing on the ground to indicate anyone had been there that day or even in the recent past. No boot treads to plaster cast, no cigarette butts to bag for DNA analysis, no cartridge cases.

I raised my sights and began to peer more closely at the small branches and sapling trunks. And patience paid off. I was good at what I did and, therefore, often lucky.

About half a foot above my head on a small birch tree I spotted a mark. A rub mark. The kind of mark a rifle might make when pressed for stability against the bark and then fired at a bird, say, or perhaps at a young man jumping repeatedly off a low raft.

Now that I was reasonably sure where the shooter had stood I looked more carefully at the bushes to the right. Sure enough, wedged in the fork of a bush, hidden from view unless you were looking very closely and knew what you might find, was a shiny brass casing. The shot that wounded Calvin Pederson was a steel-jacketed Remington center-fire .22-caliber slug. It had been fired from a rifle probably used mostly for target practice and occasionally plinking at varmints. A good shot, but not requiring expert sniper talent.

I smiled to myself, bagged the casing and got out of there. The slug itself was probably unrecoverable, but the brass just might have a fingerprint or other clue. I retrieved my vehicle and drove around to the Bartelmes' where I encountered Tod and Josie, who had just returned from the hospital and were being quizzed by a bevy of Ramsey County law officers. Calvin was awake but groggy, Josie reported, and every sign favored a full recovery.

I knew the sergeant in charge and was able to take him aside for a brief chat. I handed over the baggie with the cartridge, explained where I'd found it and departed with his thanks and a promise to stay in touch on the case. Things were definitely looking up.

In spite of a paucity of evidence, the discovery of the cartridge was going to provide me with a very large lever.

CHAPTER 10

I SPRAWLED ON MY LADY'S CARPET, staring up at her petite slacks-clad knees on the couch next to my head. "So that's the basic story. If it was just the Bartelmes' difficulties I might dismiss the whole thing as ordinary break-ins and that kind of trouble."

"Don't you think it's odd that lawyer tried to get you to quit the case?"

I smiled to myself, thinking, *Exactly, babe. The more somebody tries to make me go away, the more likely I am to stick around.*

"It's not likely that lawyer acted on his own, is it?" she went on. Her fingers trailed over the edge of the couch cushion and I nibbled at them.

"Don't think so, but the answer to that could depend on what kind of lawyer he is. I mean, is he just a functionary, doing whatever he's told or does he actively look out for his clients' interests? I don't know the man. Yet."

"I could perhaps help in that line of questions," Catherine said, leaning forward and peering over the edge of the couch at me.

"You could?"

"Sure. I have a lawyer, you know. A whole firm, in fact. Lawyers know about other lawyers. I'll ask. Discreetly, it goes without saying."

"Ah, my resources are becoming infinite," I said, raising a hand and caressing her nearest knee. "My reach is global. I am not to be denied."

"Well, don't go getting a big head over it," she giggled, pushing my hand away and getting up from the couch. "I'm making tea. Want some?"

* * * *

THE NEXT MORNING things had changed dramatically, and not for the better. When I got to my office I had two calls on the answering device. I'd ignored them at the apartment because I didn't like to bring my work home except, of course, when necessary. The earliest call came in late the previous afternoon from the lawyer, Gareth Anderson."I haven't had an answer, Mr. . . . Sean. My, ah, my client is anxious to know where we stand. I need to hear from you right away that you've declined to take Bartelmes' case. Please get back to me." *Pushy,* I thought. I wondered if Gareth was feeling a little pressure. If so, where from?

I needed to put him off for as long as possible. The longer he and his principal, whoever it was, weren't certain of my role in this affair of the Yap, the longer I had an advantage, however slight. In my business, slight advantages were sometimes all it took. A razor-thin hesitation, like that over my double name, I could sometimes parlay into a solution. Or if not that, a little protection that could occasionally keep me alive.

The other call was from St. Louis. PI Max Wisnewsky. His report suggested there indeed had been some thievery at the deceased's apartment, or condo, or house. I'd have to check on exactly what Mr. Lewis's accommodation had been. I was of the opinion that the kind of living circumstances a person had were often a clue into where and how I might uncover important information. Even in remote St. Louis. I called him back.

"What's the situation? What kind of a place did our Mr. Lewis have?"

Wisnewski hummed while he thought how to answer my question. "Small, one bedroom, no separate dining room. An apartment on the third floor. Elevator, nice middle-class building."

"Tell me about the apartment itself," I said, scribbling on a pad.

"Hard to tell now. The place was thoroughly trashed, as I mentioned."

"Yeah," I said, wishing I could see the place for myself. Maybe I'd see if the Bartelmes would pop for a quick trip to Saint Louie.

"The guy was a vet, heavily invested in world war memorabilia, and not just his own career. Pictures on the walls, lot of groups."

"Framed pictures on the walls. Lots of them." I squinted at the far wall of my office, visualizing Mr. Lewis's apartment. "Tell me more detail."

Wisnewsky sighed. "Mostly, as I said, there are group photos. You know, guys standing together under the wing of an airplane or sitting on a bunch of bombs. In fatigues, mostly. One or two with the billed dress cap, likely the pilots. Maybe a bombardier. Some of them have a legend printed on the photograph. You know the kind? Those are probably the official record pictures. They took a lot of those all over the world, you know?"

"Yes, I do know. They were all framed pictures on the walls, right?"

"Right. Under glass."

"All right." I made a note and stared at my bare wall. I ought to get some art up there. Something evocative to put clients in the right frame of mind. Catherine would help me choose. "What else?"

"Neighbors said he always carried a big key ring. Nobody has seen it. And apparently the cops in . . . where is that? Wy-no-nah? What's that, some kind of Scandinavian name?"

"Indian. Winona. Native American word," I said. "No key ring in his effects up here." I was thinking hard. "Listen, he had a box, a safe deposit box, right? It's been opened, and there's nothing much of significance, just personal papers, mementos, right?"

"Pretty much. Except for one thing."

"One thing?"

"Yeah. They found a pebble in a tiny brown paper envelope. Actually, a rough diamond."

"Really. A diamond. What's the deal?"

"It's not huge, maybe half a carat, maybe more. Local police are running it down. Not even a faint pencil mark on the envelope."

"Okay. Stay with it. I'm not sure how my client feels, but I'd like to know whatever they can discover about that rock. And do something else for me. I'd like a decent copy of each of the pictures hanging on Stan Lewis's wall."

"Big job. That'll take a while, but I can do it."

"Thanks. I'll be in touch."

It probably didn't mean anything. On the other hand, Stan Lewis was an old vet, a man who had only a high school education who joined the Army right after graduation. Here was a guy who never distinguished himself at anything. His meteoric rise in the military got him two more pay grades in almost seven years and a posting to a ground crew for an undistinguished bomber group that did nearly all its time on New London in the Pacific. After being mustered out in 1948, I knew he went home and got a succession of jobs as a maintenance guy that kept him in a reasonable way. Then he retired, never married, no kids anyone knew of. A nice ordinary veteran who did his duty and lived out a quiet life. The American Dream.

So why was he murdered on a train in Winona, Minnesota, and why did he have an uncut diamond in his safe deposit box?

I decided to call Tod Bartelme.

"Tod."

"Yeah, Sean." He sounded tired, or weary.

"How's Calvin doing?"

"Good. Getting better fast. Listen, Sean, I'm tied up here. What can I do for you?"

"I wanted to ask about Stan Lewis."

"Can it wait? Maybe later today or tomorrow sometime?"

"Normally, I'd say yes, but something's come up that may interfere with my investigation. We should talk, and I want to show you some things."

A pause while my client thought about his life at that moment. "All right. Meet me at the storage place in Maplewood at one. Will that do? I have to go there again to let the police in."

"One this afternoon. Sure. Thanks."

Not ideal, but that would work.

I sauntered down the hall to my good Swedish buddies, the Revulons. "If you have a few, I could use a search or two."

Belinda looked up from her keyboard and took a deep breath. I sometimes thought she did that consciously just to provoke me. I admired her cleavage in the neckline under her thin blouse and grinned.

"Diamonds," I said. "I need to know about diamonds. Where they come from, a little history, but mainly some sources so I can read up on the little rocks. Can do?"

"Can do. I'll bring you a printout."

I returned to my office and thought about Richard Hillier.

An hour later I was still thinking about Mr. Hillier. I knew he worked for Mr. Pederson. My information from several impeachable sources was that he did some heavy lifting for Pederson. Why was he present when I talked to the family? Had he figured there might be need for his muscle? Or did Pederson just have the man around all the time? Nobody had commented on his being at a family gathering. Maybe some people thought he was sort of part of the family.

There came a rap-rap-rapping at my office door. Not a raven. Rather the blonde Belinda entered with a fist full of printouts of stuff she'd found on the Internet. She smiled and laid them on my desk.

"Interesting stones, diamonds," she said. "I got some surprises."

"Were you discreet?"

"Always, Sean. No cookies, snacks, or tracks."

"Excellent," I said and picked up the neat pile of papers. One of the reasons I liked having Belinda or Beulah Revulon do my searching was the security factor. They had enthusiastic tricks to obscure their presence in any site, anywhere. They seemed to love detecting and then thwarting the little programs on websites designed to register your address and then send you stuff you didn't want, called cookies. Their cloaking expertise meant I was not advertising my interest in ways that might come back to bite me or my clients. It also meant it was unnecessary for me to invest in expensive and complex electronics to protect me and my clients.

The information Ms. Revulon had dredged up was indeed interesting. It seems diamonds were an ancient trade, beginning in India in a previous century. Before the Christian era, in fact. Way before. Africa got all the publicity at the moment, but it is wasn't the first nor even the primary source of diamonds in our world.

Diamonds were found in varying quantities throughout the Far East and some of the most famous and largest were from that part of the world. Today, it turned out, Australia was responsible for most of the world's diamond mining. Who knew? I reached for the telephone and dialed St. Louis again.

"Max. Me again. About that diamond. I think I want as much about its source as your intrepid dicks can discover. I don't just mean who may have sold it to Lewis, but where it was mined and how it might have come into Stan's hand. Even theories, solid or half-baked."

"I take it you're developing some theories of your own."

"Perhaps, but I don't want to jinx it."

"I get it. Later."

I hung up again thinking about an American GI who spent a lot of time in Southeast Asia during the turmoil of war. Coming home with a contraband diamond or three wouldn't be so strange. There were definitely layers to this Yap business that would have to be excavated in greater depth, as it were.

CHAPTER 11

E XPLORATION, IF NOT with spade and pick, was something I had experience with. Meanwhile, there was other business to attend to,
such as the mail, depositing incoming checks for past work, and bill
paying. So I sat at my desk and did paperwork while the sun tracked slowly
across the worn wooden planks of my office floor. There were no phone calls,
no assassination attempts. The world spun neither faster nor came to a halt.
An ordinary morning ended when I left the office to grab a fast lunch on my
way to meet Bartelme.

In Maplewood, back at the gate to the storage facility, I was accosted
with a hostile or suspicious look from the old guy at the gate. Maybe he had
a thing for short guys. Tod was already at his storage bin with the overhead
door rolled up. He was almost out of sight at the back of the space when I
arrived, muttering to himself, shoving boxes around.

"Yo, Mr. Bartelme," I called.

Silence. He was apparently frozen in place.

"Tod," I tried again, "Sean Sean here." I stepped carefully across the
sun-slammed open front of the place.

"Oh, yeah. Sorry. You startled me, I guess. Hang on."

More boxes being moved. My client appeared at one side of the space.
I put out a hand and he wiped his right on his dusty jeans and we shook.

"You seem a little jumpy."

Bartelme shrugged and mopped his face with a white hanky he ex-
tricated from the back pocket of his tight pants. "Yeah, I guess. Cal's shooting
after what happened here has really freaked me out. His mother will be arriving in a few hours."

"That's what I want to talk to you about. I did a little research. Had
some help from some of the neighbor boys. We recreated as best we could

the circumstances of the shooting." I laid out the prints I'd made on the hood of Tod's car. He was quick to see what I had seen.

"The shot must have come from across the bay." He put his finger on the picture of the brush I had examined.

"Right. The shot didn't come from inside the house." I looked him in the eye.

He looked back. "You thought it had?"

I nodded. "That thought did occur. Just as it did to you."

Tod frowned and shook his head vigorously. "No, no. Never. No one could have. Not from the house. Ridiculous."

"Sure, but you did consider it. Your relief here was apparent to me. Which tells me something. I thought about it because that's my job. That's what you hired me for. To think about all the possibilities. So c'mon, Tod, what aren't you telling me? I've felt all along there are undercurrents, stuff that isn't being talked about. All families have—what's the current phrase?—issues. Right. We don't have disagreements or conflicts or fights anymore. We have issues. At first I thought it might be Maxine. That act can be embarrassing, I agree."

"Act?" Tod interrupted.

"Sure. She turns it off and on like a light switch. Maxine's pulling your collective chains. I just don't know why. I have other questions in that arena, but first, that little grove over there." I pointed at one picture. "I went there. I looked carefully and discovered something that satisfies me that was where the shooter stood." I paused but Tod didn't ask what it was I had found. Was that significant? Or was he just burdened with a lot of other questions?

"Another thing I wanted to tell you is this," I continued. "I've had a conversation with the lawyer, Gareth Anderson. He encouraged me to refuse this case. Any idea why that is?"

Tod frowned and shook his head. "No idea. He contributed to the first trips and we've asked for more, but I don't know why he'd want you off the case."

"He's not your lawyer, correct?"

"Right. He's had Preston, Josie's dad, as a business client for years. Josie and I don't have a regular attorney. Maybe he's worried about the costs of these trips to his client."

"It's probably nothing." I shrugged. "Maybe he just doesn't like short guys. I'd appreciate it if you wouldn't mention I told you about his approach."

No reaction. I had to be careful how much I tried to influence Tod's actions going forward. I didn't want to be responsible for more mayhem. "I figure all the people I met on your deck have had some level of financial input to your wife's project. True?"

"That's right. When these incidents began to happen—the vandalism, the thefts—and we talked about hiring a detective, some of the family objected. In spite of how it maybe looks, we really aren't wealthy and it's stretching us to make these trips."

"I'm going to have separate conversations with everybody involved. I'd prefer it if you didn't alert anybody before I get to them."

Bartelme nodded. "No problem. I don't like some of them all that much, anyway."

"Where's your wife?"

He looked at me for a long moment and then said. "She's either at home or at the hospital with Cal. Cal's mother's arriving from Chicago any time. I guess I already said that, and I think Josie feels responsible. Like she didn't keep Cal safe the way his own mother would have."

"Here's something else that's interesting. Stan Lewis, the veteran you were supposed to meet?"

Tod winced and nodded. Taking responsibility for violent acts of others seemed to run in the Bartelme family. "They opened his safe deposit box and found a single uncut diamond of fairly significant size."

I stopped. I was watching Tod closely. He didn't give me anything other than mild surprise.

"Is that significant?" he asked.

"I don't know. You have any diamond jewelry?"

"Josie has a few pieces. Inherited from her mother, I think. You'll have to ask her."

"Not necessary. I take it Lewis's diamond doesn't mean anything to you."

"Nope."

I left, assuring Tod I'd check back in a day or so. When I got to the Bartelmes' house in White Bear Lake, luck smiled my way. Josie had just arrived from the hospital where she and Calvin's mother had had a tearful meeting, and the rest of the family was off the premises. We sat down in the cool living room next to the fieldstone fireplace.

"How did you come to this idea?" I asked Josie. "To try to locate your relative's remains?"

"Seems a little ghoulish, you think?"

"That wasn't my initial reaction, but I understand how some people might feel that way."

"The government has this bureau that's responsible for tracking down MIAs. Mostly they're looking for service people from Vietnam and Korea. There's a lab in Hawaii that does advanced DNA testing of remains when they're found. Various groups around the country are trying to put together detailed histories of military units. I think reunions of military units happen almost every month somewhere."

I remembered reading about the marking of the December seventh anniversary of the bombing of Pearl Harbor where American vets and Japanese vets came together in a peaceful commemoration.

"So when I began to hear a little about my relatives who had fought in World War Two, I wondered about my granduncle, Richard.

"It wasn't very strong at first, but Tod got interested too. Uncle Amundson is the only man in my family not buried in a cemetery somewhere. We have two relatives at Arlington and one in France, like a lot of families with military traditions.

"Once we'd found his record, Tod discovered there's a small group of army air force guys still alive from the same bomber group, the 350th."

"I gather you've talked with some. Did they know your granduncle?"

"Only one of them who knew him is still alive. The group was big enough that not everybody knew every other plane crew. I guess planes were shifted in and out of bomber groups, sometimes for only a few missions."

"Could be confusing, I bet. Hard to trace and hard for the guys to remember."

She smiled, tilting her head while she took a minute. "Yes. There's still a lot of conflicting information out there. A lot of the men with time on their hands wrote diaries, sometimes while they were flying the actual missions. There are contemporaneous observations and records of air combat, in my granduncle's case."

"And I guess some of them don't agree, am I right?"

"Do I sound like a lawyer?" Josie smiled. "Correct. Even more interesting, the official record, usually from the national archives, is sometimes quite different from the recollections of the guys who were there."

"But you and your husband sorted that all out."

"Yes, although we're still sorting. In the process we made contact with a lot of veterans groups and relatives of some of the people linked to the bomber group. The 350th. That's how we found Stan Lewis." Her voice broke, and she grabbed a tissue to blow her nose.

"Once your search led you to the ocean off Yap Island, what happened next?

"We talked about how to get to the islands and trying to find the plane. To dive on the site. Tod wanted to raid our retirement money and our IRAs. But I talked to my dad. He agreed to help."

"How did Tod react when you told him?"

"At first he was unhappy I'd talked to dad about it at all, but then I suggested we try to make it a family project. Richard Amundson's a relative to all of us, after all. So we wrote to everybody in my family. All the related Pedersons."

"And?"

"And they were very generous."

"Anybody in particular?"

"You mean besides my dad?" She smiled and glanced over my shoulder toward where I knew there was a handsome clock on a sideboard.

"What about your husband's family?"

"Yes. We wrote to them as well. Some of them agreed to help. A couple, who could afford it, gave quite a lot. They're all from the East Coast so we don't see them very often. That's another reason why this is so upsetting.

We've had help from lots of family members. And now that we've made contact with family and some of the living fliers, they're really interested, too."

"I can understand that. Any of the planes shot down that you find have links to families of the crews? It must be very personal for a lot of people," I said. It was beginning to look as if I might have a Cecil B. DeMille production here, a cast of thousands.

"Mr. Sean," Josie said, "Cal's being released from the hospital and his mother's bringing him here to the house for a few more days. They should be here at any time, and I still have to get a bedroom ready."

"I understand. Just one more question for now. Do you have any diamond jewelry?"

She stared at me for a moment. "What an odd question."

I explained about Stan Lewis's gem. "I don't know if it means anything one way or another. But questions are my stock in trade."

"I have some pieces I can show you at another time. I inherited them from my mother."

"Thanks. I'll call again when I have more questions." That was a foregone conclusion. We walked to the door.

Chapter 12

I LEPT INTO MY TAURUS and went looking for Richard Hillier. Preston Pederson's secretary told me he wasn't expected to be available for the rest of the day. Pederson's office suite was situated in a newish office park off the north side of Maplewood, another of the ubiquitous suburban cities that litter the landscape around our Twin Cities. There were a lot of shiny late-model Caddies and a sprinkling of exotic foreign jobs in the parking lot that extended on three sides of the glassy building.

Pederson's firm, a small brokerage with, apparently, a polished, high-buck clientele, was a player in the local and regional markets, but had remained a fairly small presence. Powerful, wealthy, but not interested in aggressive expansion. An interesting philosophy. The massive floor-to-ceiling solid dark wood door swung open easily to my pressure. The reception room was not large, nor was it opulent. The woman at the desk was about what you'd expect. She was slender, middle-aged and conservatively dressed. She had a nice smile.

I explained my business, and she offered coffee. I declined. She went away and returned in a minute to take me back to Hillier's office. It was the second one down the single hall. There were windows on the outside wall which gave one a nice view of brush, a few mature trees and in the middle distance, a small pond complete with motionless ducks. I wondered if the ducks were real and if they were captive. I hoped not, if they were real.

Hillier's office was small and plain. It wasn't a closet, but it could have been. Most offices gave you some insight into the interests or personality of the occupant. Not this one. If Hillier left, in twenty-four hours one wouldn't know who had occupied the space. There wasn't even a name on the door.

The man didn't get up from his large, black, well-padded chair behind a medium-sized double pedestal desk. He looked at me and pointed at one of two side chairs against the opposite wall. Then he waved the woman off, muttering, "Close the door. Please."

The please came as an afterthought. I wondered if he'd been told to be more polite to the office help.

She departed without a backward glance, doing as ordered. When the door snicked shut, Hillier looked at me, devoid of any expression on his tanned face. If I didn't know better, I'd have put him down as an avid golfer with plenty of wherewithal and interest in the game, a man who closed deals between chip shots and wiped out the competition after long drives into the fading sun with a heavy club.

"Mr. Sean, I have no idea how I can help you. What is it you want to know, exactly?" His voice was low and flat.

"I'm not sure. What, exactly do you do around here?" It was not a polite question.

Hillier didn't react except to lean back in his chair and nod once, as if I'd just confirmed something he'd expected. I was sure my impertinence would not go unreported, which I expected. Others down the line might prepare for what never came their way, which just might give me a little edge. So I was pushy with this man. Not expecting an answer, I moved on.

"Tod and Josie have provided me with an overall view of their financial arrangements for these trips to Yap Island, but I need to confirm a few details."

"I don't see how that can help you. What does that have to do with whoever is trying to disrupt their trips?"

"Trust me, right now no detail is too small to be overlooked."

"Yeah, right."

"So, how much have you invested in this enterprise"

"That is none of your damn business."

"Of course not." I smiled at him. "But it will help me to know."

"I can hardly care less what will or won't help you, *Mister* Sean. So just forget it."

"I gather your employer's worried about his daughter in this regard. Doesn't it bother you at least a little that your lack of cooperation could jeopardize my investigation?"

Hillier's response was a snort and a slight shake of the head. He sat there in front of me at his bare-topped desk, in smug self-righteousness. He was almost daring me to get some useful information out of him.

"How long have you worked for Mr. Pederson?"

"I don't work for Mr. Pederson."

"No?"

"No. I'm employed by Pederson Investments."

I raised one eyebrow. The left one. I couldn't seem to get the same response out of the other one.

"But Mr. Pederson is the sole owner of PI, correct?"

He shrugged. "I wouldn't know."

"So, what is it you do around here?" I glanced around with an elaborate smile on my face. As if to point out there was nothing in the office, or on his desk, that would suggest any kind of task of any sort. "What's your title?" Because Pederson Investments was a private investment company, the only information I'd located was a brief puff piece designed to lead people with wads of idle cash to trust the firm to invest it wisely in high-yield properties and building projects. Who was employed at the firm and for what purpose was hidden from casual view. There were rumors, however.

"My sources say you're the muscle." I smiled and spread my hands. I hoped the effect was ingenuous. "If tenants need to be brought into line, to sign the quit claim deed or just vacate the premises when needed, I hear you can be very persuasive."

Hillier didn't smile back, but he didn't frown or swear at me, either. "Sometimes, in this business, we have to do things that are uncomfortable. A tenant refuses to leave, even after legit termination of the lease. Or we sometimes get freeloaders moving in and giving us hassle. That's where those lies come from, Mr. Sean. Our company is very careful of our well-deserved clean reputation. Don't believe everything you hear." He glanced at his watch. "And I'm sorry to say, I have an appointment on the other side of town. So you'll have to excuse me."

Hillier rose and extended a big paw across the desk. Slick. I wasn't going to just sit there in his empty office and pout, was I?

I shook his hand and left, knowing I hadn't laid a glove on the man. Not a ripple, not a rise. I would have to pursue other lines of inquiry until I had something substantial to club him with.

CHAPTER 13

ALTHOUGH YOU MIGHT not realize it from reading a lot of detective fiction these days, most private investigators had more than one client on the hook at one time. Since most of us got paid after the case closed, and retainers, as we like to call 'em, never quite cover ongoing expenses anyway, we needed more than a single case going at once.

This was particularly true for single practitioners like my humble self. Most big law firms, where a large number of referrals originated, were careful with their cash and didn't like to pay for idle hands. Not every case required a crackerjack investigator, so even my most regular client, Harcourt, Saint Martin, Saint Martin, Jove, et cetera, et cetera, was willing to put up with the small inconvenience of not having me at their beck and call.

So, while I was immersing myself in the intricacies of Bartelme-Pederson, I had other irons in the fire, so to speak. Tonight I was dealing with one of those irons. It required me to dress up. No red Converse this evening. No, tonight was shiny patent-leather shoes and a lightweight suit, a black-tie affair, which gave me a small problem.

I was glad I wasn't doing security at a full formal event, the kind where the men wear white bow ties and tails. And white gloves. Being a short fellow, white tie and tails makes me dangerously penguin-esque. That makes me cranky. Some Emperor penguins, I'd been advised, reached six feet in height, whereas I was five-two on a good day.

So, anyway, tonight I was being a security guard for a gala affair at a posh country club in one of the Westside golf club bunkhouses. I didn't actually know this particular mansion-like club house had bedrooms, but some do and the size of this place, with its large and small meeting rooms, a good-sized ballroom and three bars associated with two dining rooms, well, you get the picture. Why not have a few private suites for the wheels who wanted to be away from home for a time?

It appeared that just having a gathering of one's two or three hundred closest friends for an evening of fun and frivolity wasn't enough attraction in the modern era, so themes or special considerations entered the picture. In this case, a local jeweler was displaying a traveling exhibition of fine and expensive designer jewelry. One of the top local bands had been engaged to provide dancing music in the big ballroom, a string trio would offer quieter music for listening in a different room and so on. I understood the attendees were even being encouraged to open their vaults and strongboxes to allow proper adornment of the attending ladies in their personal jewelry.

So bling bling. In great and expensive quantities. For that, you needed security. The folks who staged these charity affairs didn't want goons in monkey suits standing around looking uncomfortable. They wanted to feel secure, but they weren't partial to uniforms. They did want security personnel reasonably well turned out, who could put words together in complete sentences, and who were competent in event of crisis. For example, if a female guest tripped and fell, they would assist her back to her feet without any unnecessary pawing of her body.

Enter Sean Sean and four others, circumspect and discreet gentlemen all. In most cases, the guests with whom we might interact would not realize they were socializing with men packing heat. Yes, we went armed. Which was a problem for me. My handgun of choice was an older model Colt .45-caliber semiautomatic—sizeable and it weighed a lot. When on the rare occasion I had to drag it out, it got immediate respect.

"Not carrying your cannon tonight, I see," commented Catherine, watching me dress. She knew this because the special rig I had for the Colt was nowhere to be seem.

"Nope. This suit isn't tailored for it. I'll carry the little .38 liteweight."

"The ankle holster," she said. Catherine went to the closet and opened her built-in safe. As our time together lengthened, she'd become, if not entirely comfortable, at least resigned to the presence of my weapons in our apartment. Not the shotguns. She drew the line at "those ugly things," as she put it.

Now she took out the soft black calfskin ankle holster and the box with the tiny short-barreled Smith and Wesson five-shot revolver the holster was designed to hold. I didn't like wearing the thing but tonight it was my only option. "You sure I don't walk funny with this thing?" I said, hiking up my pant leg. I'd had the pant leg slightly enlarged to accommodate the holster and make it easier to get at the weapon.

"No funnier than usual." She grinned down at me.

* * * *

THE CLUB HAD BEEN built on the side of a hill between the front nine and the back nine, so there wasn't a real front-back orientation. At the upper, smaller, parking area where I parked, one could unload golf clubs from the trunk and in a few steps place the bag in the carrier of the golf cart you'd already reserved, waiting at the edge of the pavement. You could even book a driver for the cart. To my left was a single-story stone-faced utility building covered with some sort of vine. Behind that a fenced enclosure held two clay tennis courts. I had no doubt the top of the nets at the center of the span was precisely thirty-six inches, tournament height, from the ground. A breezeway led to the main structure. Here one entered at the third floor and then went by elevator or stairs to upper floors, straight through to the main ballroom, or downstairs to one of the bars or restaurants, the small gymnasium and workout center, the locker rooms and the parking area for other golf carts.

I was arriving almost ninety minutes early, and the sun was still sending heat onto the broad fairways and greens that surrounded the club. The fairways were green, indicating the use of a fair amount of water. My feet got warm just strolling across the asphalt parking lot. It was my habit to arrive early in order to check out the layout and refresh my memory of hallways, stairs and doors. I liked to become aware of any alterations since I last trod those thick, dark green carpets.

I went in and introduced myself to the head honcho, a tall (to me) well set-up fellow with clean, properly trimmed fingernails, short hair, and shiny black shoes. He checked me off on a typed roster of names and offered to accompany me on a tour of the clubhouse. I declined with thanks.

After I wandered around the halls and poked into a few nooks and blind cul-de-sacs, I went to the big ballroom where the main action would happen this night. The first thing that attracted my eyes was the view. The tall windows on the east wall looked out on the golf course and a pretty special sight it was, lit by the lowering golden evening sun. The angle of view was such that the city skyline was invisible. We could have been on Mars. Well, probably not. Voices attracted me so I sauntered over to one corner where the traveling exhibition was being arranged in several long glass cases set on wooden trestles. The trestle sawhorses were concealed under long folds of heavy white and pale rose-colored velvet drops. The cases were glass on three sides to allow maximum viewing. I looked closely and discovered that the tops could be opened, but they had small, well-concealed locks in the corners to reduce any chance of pilfering. Three young women in white shirts with short black skirts, black hose, and black high heels busily touched up the display. Small pin spots had been artfully arranged to send strong glints zinging off the polished jewels.

I introduced myself to the man obviously in charge. He in turn introduced me to his security chief, a large black dude with a brilliant smile of shiny white teeth. He smiled a lot and shook my hand without a macho display of finger strength, which I appreciated.

The sun went down, and the attendees began to arrive. Some of them came in rented limos, some in their personal, highly polished Caddies, BMWs, Benzes, and Lincolns. It truly was a gala affair, as the society lady from the *Star Tribune* would later dub it in her column. She was elegantly turned out, I thought, clutching the arm of a handsome fellow I didn't recognize.

My job, unless a problem arose, was actually quite easy. Security was expected, and single men standing around ogling guests was fine. There was plenty to ogle. Most of the women were seriously decked out. Long dresses predominated although some of the younger women with good legs wore short, tight skirts. Décolletage was on display. Ample bosoms adorned with jewelry passed my gaze in serried review. The dances were mostly waltzes and fox trots, as befitted the age and comportment of the guests. Although the bar was well attended through the entire evening and did a persistent business, I detected no social lapses. Then a woman I hadn't seen before walked by in a theatrical costume of yards of deep burgundy velvet. The dress, which trailed behind her on the floor, had a wide neckline and sleeves that just rested on the ends of her shoulders—not quite a strapless gown.

She must have entered by a different door. Her brilliant white hair framed her face with soft ringlets. Although she was clearly into her sixth decade, she wore her years well, and I could see she was someone used to the power and prestige her wealth afforded her. As she passed, our eyes caught and she smiled. I nodded, reflecting that her smile had seemed genuine, not that of a superior being. But she radiated position and power. I was reminded of the wife of Ephraim Harcourt, a woman I had sent to jail a few years earlier. She had generated a similar kind of power when she cared to.

I knew I had not seen this woman before. I suspected she'd be interesting to talk to. My snap judgment was based on far too little evidence, but there you are. There was more. Resting on her chest just above the beginning of her cleavage was a large and elaborate necklace. Several oval red stones I took to be rubies rested in complicated settings that might have been platinum or white gold, all linked together around the center stone. This rock, perhaps five or six carats, was intense yellow, and it sparkled and almost sang aloud in the muted hubbub of the room.

I'd recently read a bit about yellow diamonds. They were among the rarest and most expensive, especially when bearing few flaws and cut to perfect dimensions. I was willing in that moment to bet that rock was almost flawless. I wished Catherine was there to see it.

The woman passed on by and I went back to my job, circulating slowly, watching the ebb and flow of the crowd, wishing I could get rid of my ankle holster because the skin under the strap was starting to itch. I turned around to go the other way, and there she was again, one hand extended as if she'd been about to pluck at my sleeve. Turned out, she had.

"Mr. Sean," she said. Her voice was mid-range, her diction precise, and she showed no hesitation in dealing with my name. Cool.

"Yes, ma'am," I responded. "You have the advantage of me."

"Yes, I do. I would like to speak to you privately for a few minutes."

"I'm afraid I can't leave the ballroom right now. Perhaps—"

"No, that's all right. If you'd bring me a martini to that table over there?" She handed me her empty glass and indicated a small, empty table for two beside one wall. "Shaken, not stirred, if you please." She smiled and turned away.

I got rid of her glass and found one of my security fellows. "I'm going to take a quick break, but I'll be right there," I said, pointing at the table. He nodded. I acquired the requested martini—shaken, not stirred—and took it to her along with a glass of ginger ale for me.

The woman smiled her thanks, gave me her fingers, and said, "Thank you. I'm Madeline Pryor."

I knew that name, but from what?

"Josie Bartelme is an associate at my husband's law firm. She's told me about their Pacific quest and the current troubles they're having. It was my husband who recommended you."

"I see. Thank your husband for that."

"It's an intriguing situation, isn't it?"

"Yes, and I'm sure you know I can't discuss it with you."

Madeline Pryor nodded and said, "Of course not. But when I realized who you were, I wanted to meet you. Then I saw you admiring my diamond." She touched it with a single finger.

"So it isn't paste, is it."

She chuckled. "I've heard you sometimes have a sharp tongue. The diamond is quite real."

"It's truly magnificent," I acknowledged.

"Yes, it is. My family's owned it for many years. The stone's been slightly altered since my family acquired it. Recut, you see."

I didn't, but it was apparent she had a point to make.

"Yes, it is now a near replica of the Moon of Baroda. Of course that yellow is larger, almost twenty-four carats, I believe."

"Truly."

She nodded, a tiny smile playing about her mouth. "Marilyn Monroe wore the Moon to the premiere of *Gentlemen Prefer Blondes*."

"Interesting. That would have been back in the 1950s somewhere."

"1953, to be precise," Mrs. Pryor went on. She sipped her martini and nodded approvingly.

"Do you know where your diamond came from?" I asked.

"Yes, a relation found the necklace in a shop in Singapore right at the end of the war. It was damaged and not as complete as this." She raised her hand and touched the diamond. "We've been given to understand this diamond was found in Borneo or perhaps in India, sometime in the late nineteenth century. There are many legends attached to precious stones. But I'm sure you're aware of that. After a few years my relative was able to have the necklace restored."

I glanced at my watch and said, "I have to get back to work."

"I hope you will be able to help Josie and Tod. To that end, if there is anything you find you need . . ." she gestured.

"Thank you, Mrs. Pryor, I'll remember your generous offer." I rose from my chair, and then leaned over and said, "May I assume you have already helped Mrs. Bartelme in her efforts to find her granduncle?"

"You may."

"Have a pleasant evening, Mrs. Pryor." I smiled and returned to my tasks. *Well, now. Another source of money shows up.* I wondered why neither Josie nor Tod happened to mention the Pryor connection. Wheels within wheels. More questions. Marilyn Monroe. My, my.

Chapter 14

AX WISNEWSKI CALLED my office. His message said he'd managed to have the pictures copied, and they were in the mail. He also said new information might warrant another call. Josie Bartelme had also phoned to ask me to come to her home that afternoon, if I could, to meet some others helping with the Yap project.

I returned Josie's call and said I would get out to White Bear Lake in the early afternoon. While I was on the blower with my client, I contemplated my shoes. I found a small smudge on the white toe of one of my red Keds. The ones with white soles. So I went to my closet and pulled out a new, clean pair. I'd take the others home and wash them.

Wisnewski answered his phone in the midst of the second ring. "Wisnewski," he said.

"Sean," I responded.

"First or last?" he said.

"Your choice. What's up?"

"I think I told you the pictures are copied and in the mail. The new information is that the crime scene people here have now been over everything they can find connected to Mr. Lewis. There's not much to say. Except for what isn't here."

"Meaning what?" I asked.

"It appears somebody removed a quantity of material from a file cabinet Lewis kept in his bedroom."

"Did he have an office?"

"Not in his apartment and not anywhere else, unless he was super careful about keeping it separate from the rest of his life so nobody's located it yet."

"Why would he do that?"

"Exactly. Of course, something might turn up, like a landlord seeing Lewis's picture or obit in the paper and remembering a tenant. Or maybe a lease runs out and the cops are called. But that's a real long shot. And, as I say, there's zero evidence he had a separate place of any sort."

"So, a dead end."

"Yeah, I'm afraid so, except for the gap in his files. Ol' Steve was a meticulous guy, so the gap in the folders is pretty obvious."

"Any hope of finding what might be missing?"

"Prob'ly not except for what we can glean from the gap. There's no "B" file folder and no "W.""

"Huh," I said. "B as in bomber group and W as in maybe war or world war. I suppose somebody snooped in P as for Pacific, or even Y?"

"Correct. Those files are accounted for. From the spaces left, it looks like there was enough there to fill a small briefcase."

"Okay. Thanks. Send me your bill. I think we're done unless something turns up here or in Winona."

I dialed the Winona PD and connected to the detective in charge of Stan Lewis's murder investigation. When I related my conversation with Wisnewski, he already had the info, but I could tell he was pleased I'd promptly called him. "There was no briefcase. No other kind of carrying case, either. So if he had those files with him, the killer copped 'em. I have to tell you, Sean, this is shaping up for the cold case cupboard."

"What's going to be the disposition of his body?"

"He's a vet. Arrangements are being made to bury him at Fort Snelling, since he has no ties to St. Louis anymore. It's the closest veterans cemetery."

"Have somebody let me know when, will you?"

We severed the connection. I had an itchy feeling I might talk only once more to that detective, and it wouldn't be about the solution to his murder case. It'd be at a funeral.

I tied the laces on my new tennis shoes and went to lunch. I had just enough time to eat and get myself out to White Bear Lake. Maybe I'd get lucky and be able to interview Alvin and his sexpot wife, Maxine, after I talked with Josie.

* * * *

MY MEDIUM-RARE STEAK sandwich with a side of *au gratin* potatoes and a crisp salad had set me up for another long day of doing what I did best, interviewing folks to try to entice from them relevant and truthful information. The day was hot and the air conditioner in the Taurus had all it could do to keep me from melting into a puddle like the Wicked Witch of the West.

The heat and humidity eased somewhat out in the suburb, but a thermometer tacked to a fence post beside the Bartelmes' garage registered in the low nineties. Josie came to the door. She was wearing green flip-flops and a wrap over what I guessed was a bathing suit. She looked as if she'd been in the sun. I could detect the aroma of some kind of sunscreen on her.

"I apologize for the casual way I'm dressed. My girlfriends, the other Js, dropped over. We've been swimming and just hanging out."

"'S'all right. I think I'd like to meet your buddies, anyway." Tod had mentioned to me Josie had two close friends from college, both with first names starting with the letter J. "How's Cal doing?"

Josie wrinkled her forehead briefly. "Fine, I guess. His mother took him away after he was released from the hospital, you know. I haven't really talked with him since then."

"I have an impression you think his mother blames you a little for his wounding."

She nodded. "I think so. She was never very supportive of our trips to Yap. She thinks there's a connection. Why don't we go out on the deck? I have a pitcher of sangria, and you can meet my friends." Josie led me through the kitchen and slid open the sliding door that led to the lakeside deck, smaller than the more protected deck where I'd first met her family. A burst of feminine laughter was quickly suppressed as we came into view.

The women seated at the small, oblong, plastic deck table were dressed in similar fashion to Josie, and bright two-piece swimsuits showed their glistening bodies to good advantage. One was dark, with clean tan lines that appeared on her bosom when she raised one hand as we approached. Her other hand grasped a tall, sweating glass of the same-colored liquid visible in a large pitcher and the other glass on the table. Sangria, I presumed.

"Oh, here's our intrepid investigator, I bet." This woman's voice carried normal Minnesota accents and tonality. She had good teeth and a nice smile. Her short dark hair gave off red highlights when she moved. "I'm Julie. Julie Walcott. This is Jennifer Alstock."

I smiled and nodded. Josie, Julie, and Jennifer. Three Js. "And I'm Sean Sean. Happy to meet you both." Jennifer Alstock was blonde, slender to the point of anorexia and looked a little nervous. Her perfunctory smile flickered on and off like a light in a bad socket and as soon as I released her fingers, she crossed her arms over her small bosom and looked away.

Josie poured me a glass of the sangria and sat down. "Sean asked to meet anybody close to us," she said, "and you guys are closer than my sister." Both women nodded.

I took a sip of sangria. It was strong. I felt the sweat beginning to form on my brow and in my crotch. Even in the shade of the umbrella overhead.

"Are we suspects?" asked Julie.

"No," I responded, "but I understand you two have been there all the while this project has developed."

"Yes," said Jennifer in a soft voice. "From the beginning."

"Since that's true, I want to get your impressions. Anything you can remember may be helpful." I turned to Josie, who recalled the first few conversations they'd all had about her granduncle and sort of set the stage.

"I'm interested in anything, everything you two can recall, particularly whatever you remember about the initial responses or concerns from the people Josie and Tod were talking to. Anything, however insignificant it may seem."

"I don't feel comfortable accusing anybody," Jennifer whispered.

"I don't expect or want you to say anything against anybody. I'm more interested in your perceptions of the interest or lack thereof as the project developed. And let me assure you this conversation is private. I would never reveal any of this to anyone else."

We talked for about an hour. Gradually Jennifer relaxed and participated more. She turned out to be the more perceptive of the two Js in her observations. She told us she thought Josie's dad was really against the thing from the beginning and even now, although he had financed a good portion of the expenses, his was a reluctant contribution.

"You really think Dad doesn't want us to keep on?" Josie asked.

"It's my impression, but I don't really know, hon. I haven't talked with your dad about this in months, but at first it was obvious he thought it was a bad idea."

"Gary Anderson, the lawyer?" interjected Julie. He talked to John, my husband, and me and tried to talk us out of contributing."

John? Great, another J.

"You never mentioned that," Josie said.

"Well, we figured he was talking for your dad, and I didn't want to get between you two." She shrugged.

"What about Alvin and Maxine?" I asked.

A moment of silence ensued. The Js looked at each other. Simultaneously all three got the giggles, helped no doubt by the constant flow of sangria. At some point, Josie went to the kitchen to fetch another big pitcher of the stuff. I was taking it easy, knowing I had to drive home. Plus I needed to keep my memory functioning so my notes of this session would be as complete as possible. I knew the little recorder running silently in my pocket wouldn't provide a real clear recording. I wasn't writing down any notes either. I was afraid either the recorder or scribbling might spook the two Js.

"Well, Alvin and Maxine." Julie took a big swallow and produced a small belch, causing Jennifer to smile. "Maxine is really okay. She just tries too hard. I mean, nice body, great jugs and all that, but she acts so predatory. She's no dummy."

Josie nodded. "That's right, but she didn't want Alvin to contribute much on our trip. She was supportive, thought it was an exciting idea at first. But when Tod started talking about money, Alvin offered a pretty large contribution right away, but Maxine was more cautious. She wanted a lot of specific details. I think Alvin would've put up a lot more money but she held him back."

"What about the lawyer," I asked. "You said he called you?" I was addressing Julie, who was giving me serious stress vibes.

She nodded. "Yeah, he talked to John, like I said, but I was in the room. It was pretty obvious he wanted us to stay out of it. I don't think he understood the dynamics of our relationship. He kept saying we didn't have a chance of ever getting our money back, no matter what was found.

"John kept saying he knew that, but that his wife, that would be me, and Josie, were close and of course he'd support me." She grinned at me. "He always does."

I nodded my understanding. I thought she was getting a little high. "What about Hillier? He doesn't seem to fit in anywhere."

All three women nodded. "Creepy," Julie contributed. "I never understood why your dad puts up with him."

Josie frowned at us.

"Wait a moment," I interposed. "I was under the impression Mr. Hillier just worked for Pederson. Is that wrong?"

Josie shook her head. "That's true, he does. But the relationship is more complicated than that. It's—I don't know. It's hard to explain, and I guess I don't understand all of it."

"He's a real letch, you know." Julie's voice was low and slurred just a little. She looked away, out toward the lake shimmering quietly in the sun. There was silence on the deck for several minutes, broken only by the restless, random sounds of small flying insects chittering on the edges of the deck and occasionally dive bombing us. A narrow-bodied bluish thing sometimes called a darning needle whined through the silence, diverted around the edge of the umbrella, paused a microsecond, and then darted off.

Julie opened her lips as if to say something, then stopped. She sipped her drink and hesitated again. I glanced at the other women, who seemed to have drawn together in a psychic barrier as if to protect each other.

Then Julie went on in a quiet, reflective tone, "I admit I was drinking more than I should have that night. Remember, Josie? John was gone somewhere and I was here alone. I kind of crashed your party."

Josie leaned forward and took her friend's limp fingers. "Hey, c'mon, sweetie, you don't have to do this. It has nothing to do with our troubles."

On the other side of the table, Jennifer Alcott stared at her friend, the glass of sangria held halfway between her mouth and the table. It was apparent whatever had happened between Julie and Hillier was news to her as well.

Julie swiveled her head toward me. I thought I saw tears in her eyes. "This what you want, to shame us? Wade around in our little improprieties? So I was a little tipsy. So maybe I flirted with 'im a little. It was harmless. I thought. Sort of. But he, he . . ." she hiccupped and stopped.

Josie grimaced, looked at me then back at Julie. "It was a big party. We had a lot of people, and they were all over the place. I couldn't keep track of everybody."

"Were you supposed to?" I asked. Seemed like a reasonable question. I could see she was taking some of the responsibility for what had happened, whatever it was.

"I was in the kitchen. I heard raised voices, a shout or something. Tod was down by the lake. There was a small crowd around the door to the bedroom behind the dining room. I went in and found Hillier and Julie. They both looked . . . I don't know, distraught. Disheveled. Julie was on her knees on the floor, and there was a big red mark on Hillier's cheek. Where she'd slapped him. There was an overturned chair beside the desk. I guess she fell off it, or something.

"I took Julie upstairs and put her to bed in the guest room. When I got back downstairs, Hillier was gone, and everybody else was on to other things. The next morning Julie told me he put his hands on her and got angry when she tried to get him to stop."

Josie looked uncomfortable and seemed ready to go on, however reluctantly. I noticed Jennifer seemed to have withdrawn from the conversation and had found things off the deck to look at.

I held up my hand. "I get the picture. You don't have to say any more."

A few minutes later Jennifer took Julie into the house, and I took my leave. At the door Josie said, "We've never talked about it. It was two years ago. I never even told Tod. I guess I didn't see the point."

"If you want some advice, don't tell him now. It probably has nothing to do with present events. But you might try getting Julie into a program."

I walked through the late afternoon sun to my car thinking about this conversation and about Richard Hillier. Talking with the three Js had evolved into a kind of rhythmic piece, like a dance or a fencing match. Thrust, parry, lunge, withdraw. There was more there than had been revealed. There were more dimensions to Mr. Hillier I hadn't yet probed. How, exactly, he fit still wasn't clear, but I calculated that, one way or another, I'd figure it out.

CHAPTER 15

THE NEXT MORNING I still hadn't figured everything out except it was clearer to me that two of the three Js and Mr. Hillier had some connection at least partially hidden. Maybe he'd come on to Jennifer as well as to Julie, only she wouldn't talk about it at all, even after a few drinks. Maybe not. Whatever it was, I had to set it aside for the nonce.

Next on my agenda was the kingpin of the group, Preston Pederson. He'd contributed the most money to the risky enterprise his only daughter was heavily involved with. It stood to reason he was the most important of the investors both from a financial as well as a familial perspective. So it was also interesting he seemed to be the most insubstantial presence so far. The discussions about the development of the Yap project seemed not to include Preston's opinions. Why not? I would prepare more thoroughly than usual.

What I learned from Internet and private sources was frustrating. There seemed to be gaps. Preston's father, Derek, had been a small contractor in St. Paul in the 1930s. He never had any major projects, but he was frequently a subcontractor. My research told me Pederson's father had build garages and additions to homes such as porches, driveways, things like that.

When he retired sometime in the 1960s, his son stepped in, having already been working for Dad. He began a rapid expansion of the business. It was apparently a heady, go-go time in construction. Preston Pederson soon became a player. He expanded into investment banking. Okay, so the old man must have done something right. If Preston was clean, what about his father?

It took me a couple days of intensive research. I was at the library a lot. I talked with some old-timers I met one night in a place on Payne Avenue. It had been called the Payne Reliever back in the day. Why was I in the Payne Reliever? Well, I knew some people who knew some other people and they had allowed while I was kicking around a different case that people at the PR pretty much knew about things on the East Side.

These two old guys, Abe and Tommy, had worked for Preston's dad as kids. They were over the hill, but they got away from the nursing home in the next block every couple of weeks in the summer to sidle on down to the old PR for a brew or two.

The bar wasn't crowded and of course it wasn't smoky, not since the state passed the ban on smoking in enclosed public places. Good for everybody's health, especially the people who worked in those bars, but it sure depressed the atmosphere you sometimes read about in Chandler or in those Black Mask detective stories. Never mind. Tommy and Abe were comfortably ensconced at one end of the long bar when I swung through the door at the other end of the room.

They wore overalls and were both seriously overweight. I suspected their livers were probably on their last legs from battling the effects of too many beers, too few antioxidants and, lately, too much sedentary existence.

"Can I buy you fellows a beer?" I inquired, sliding onto a stool next to them.

"You that Sean fella?" Abe looked me up and down, probably to satisfy himself. What he saw was my slender, well-shaven self in jeans and a short-sleeved, checkered cotton shirt, and red Keds with clean white soles.

The bartender, a tall chick with red-and-blue streaked hair, a nice figure and a pleasant smile, was right there to take my order for three drafts. We all chose Miller.

"Sure would be good to taste a Hamm's again," I said, nodding at a faded Hamm's Beer sign above the back bar. I was shameless when necessary. I'd never in my life seen a Hamm's Beer, much less tasted one.

Abe smirked and took a long swallow that disposed of most of the contents of his glass in one long gulp. He wiped his mouth with the back of his hand. Tommy shook his head, saluted me with his glass and poured a goodly portion down his gullet. He smiled with satisfaction.

"So, what can we do for ya, young fella?" he asked quietly.

"I'm a private detective. I'm doing a little research on Pres Pederson's old man, Derek, and his construction company. I turned up your names on a short list of employees back in the fifties and sixties."

"Yep. And if I ask you what this is all about, you're gonna say its confidential and you can't talk about it, right?" He took another drink from his glass and shifted on the stool. Abe was grinning at me over Tommy's big shoulder. "An' then you're gonna say it's nothing special and not to worry, nobody's going to get messed up or nothing, right?"

I stared at Tommy.

Abe punched Tommy on the shoulder and chortled. "You been readin' those detective novels again, aintcha, Tommy?"

"You don't say," I said, sipping my own beer. "Who do you read? I'm sort of partial to Shel Scott, myself."

"I like this guy in Florida, Hiaasen? And there's this Crider fellow down in Texas. He tells a pretty good western sort of story."

So we spent a few minutes comparing notes on the detective stories we'd read. He didn't know about James Burke, so I wrote down the name for him. Then we got around to something real. To Preston Pederson.

The boys told me a lot of tales that might or might not have been true, or partly true. Or partly legend. Both men had a good time reliving a stronger, more pleasant past that might have lost or gained something over the passage of time.

"So did anything ever happen that seemed odd or different, back then?"

Tommy shrugged and gestured for another beer. But Abe looked thoughtful and then he nudged his buddy. "You remember when Pres cleaned out the office that time?"

Tommy grinned and said, "Oh, yeah. He'd been on us about not keeping the site clean. I don't remember exactly when it was. But Pres, he got kinda ticked at the old man, so late one day he grabs a broom and starts tearing around and cleaning up the trailer we had on the site. It was somewhere over by Phalen, I think.

"Anyways we kinda got in the spirit of things and helped him. We threw out a bunch of stuff and swept the floors and sh—stuff like that."

Abe nodded and picked up the thread. He got a big smile on his face. "The old man showed up the next morning, and it was pretty good until he found that old cruddy box in the corner was gone. Well, we couldn't remember if it had been thrown out with the rest of the trash. There was never nothin' in it, I 'member, except mebby some coarse gravel or pebbles in the corners. Some other trash. You know."

"Gravel," I said.

"Yeah, the old man grabbed Pres, and they went out to where we had dumped the trash. He wouldn't let us help, but he was swearing a blue streak. They went through that big pile of stuff for a long time and got kinda dirty in the bargain."

Tommy burped softly and said, "I never found out what they were looking for. Maybe nothing? Anyway, after that we never cleaned up the trailer, ever again."

After that, the conversation wound down. Tommy and Abe weren't up to a long night of beer drinking and tale telling anymore, although it was clear they still had memories and faint hopes. I hung in until they both called it a night. Then I put the boys in a cab and sent them two blocks to their retirement home.

Gravel. Pebbles in St. Louis and gravel in Saint Paul. We were still a long way from Yap.

CHAPTER 16

P RESTON PEDERSON DIDN'T fit my new image of him. Of course, we'd already met at his daughter's house in our initial confrontation. I know, we didn't have hard words or anything, but it had felt like a certain contest of wills started there. Then there was that image called up by Tommy and Abe of Pres Pederson as a youngster with ready fists and a hard-scrabble background in his dad's hardhat construction operation. I'd had a pretty good look at Tommy's hands during our barroom conversation. Along with the inroads of age and arthritis, Tommy's left was missing the tip of the little finger, and he had favored the left when he hoisted his beer glass. The light glistened off the slick scar tissue on the back of his hand, a hand that had seen hard use.

Now, I eased into a comfortable side chair across from Pederson in his well-appointed inner sanctum. It had taken quite an effort to get in here. And I had an appointment. I arrived at the appropriate time to find I had to work my way through three layers of attendants. Harder even than reaching the inner workings of my favorite firm of legal eagles, Harcourt, Bryce, St. Martin, St. Martin, et cetera.

I wasn't clear what, exactly, those attendants did here at Pederson Construction and Investments, Incorporated. But they were nice eye candy. So was the place. Long hallways with rich wooden paneling, plush carpet, subdued activity, everything one would expect in a nice, successful Midwestern firm. So why did the faint odor of decay or something like it reach my bullshit detector?

Preston Pederson's corner office in a Saint Paul office building that overlooked Mears Park was as comfortable and tasteful as the maze of offices and hallways I'd just been conducted through. "Good to see you again, Sean," Pederson hazarded. "I hope your investigation is proceeding well?" We'd shaken hands briefly. His was still hard, a reminder of his construction background.

"Well enough, I'd say." I adjusted the creases in my pants so the knees wouldn't bag. Then I crossed my legs and grinned at him. "Nice digs you have here. I expect your dad would be quite proud, considering the construction trailer he usually worked out of."

"I understand. You've been checking me out. All of us, I suppose. Nobody can be completely anonymous anymore, what with the Internet and ever-more-sophisticated means of examining the private lives and backgrounds of just about anyone. Right? Even you, Mr. Sean."

I nodded. "Even me. I'd give you the standard rundown, but I bet I wouldn't be telling you things you don't know."

"Fascinating woman, Catherine Mckerney. It happens there may have been a connection there." He waved one hand, palm out in a casual fashion, barely lifting his wrist from the desk. "Oh, nothing sinister, I assure you. Investments, you know." His smile was a trifle wolfish, I thought.

"I'm talking to just about everyone with any connection to the case, however remote," I said. "Things are a little more complicated, though, with the murder of that gentleman from St. Louis."

"Murder." Pederson's eyebrows flew up, practically all the way to his hairline. "I hadn't heard. Can you tell me anything about it?"

So I told him about the murder of man on the train from St. Louis, a veteran of the Second World War who was on his way to see Tod and Josie about their search for Richard Amundson.

Pederson didn't waste any sympathy on the dead vet. "Did this Lewis fellow know Amundson?"

"Don't have an answer to that. Did you?"

"What?"

"Know your uncle?" I hadn't worked out the relative ages. Pederson was certainly alive during the war.

"Er, no, I don't think I did. His family lived in Wisconsin. Near Madison, if I recall. But this Lewis, what do we know about him?"

I related what I knew, at least, everything I thought would interest Pederson. I somehow neglected to mention the results of my active inquiries in St. Louis. He would likely be very interested in those facts, but I wasn't ready to lay out all my cards to the man. By now I was forming a little theory of this case, and it tentatively pointed to Pederson as the possible thorn in the ointment. Or the burr under Tod's saddle. Why that would be was another question. Because I figured if Pederson just withdrew his financial support, some others would follow. That would most likely end his daughter's quest. Maybe Pederson was afraid of alienating his daughter so he was using this underhanded method of torpedoing the quest. Family dynamics were always convoluted and frequently hard to sort out, which was one reason I didn't do divorces. Give me a nice clean street robbery or random serial killer any time.

Anyway, he seemed to maintain an active interest in my tales. "I take it this detective in Winona hasn't any real leads."

"That's true, but they'll continue to investigate. There's no statute of limitations on murder."

"In fact, they don't have any information to connect this man to either Josie or my son-in-law. Correct?"

"Right, although the cops know he was on his way to see Tod and Josie. He hadn't traveled anywhere outside St. Louis in the past dozen years—he was old—so there's certainly a connection there," I said. "But I don't expect they'll be getting up your nose. Although I do think Tod and Josie will get a call or a visit, if the detective is thorough. Or if they turn up something that leads them up the tracks to White Bear."

He glanced at me. I don't think he cared for my image of a Winona detective sauntering up the railroad tracks. Pederson showed me some impatience then. He glanced at the clock in a silver case that stood on a low nearby shelf. It didn't have numbers, just small silver bars arrayed in a classic circle outside a pair of black hands, forefingers extended.

He shifted in his chair and said, "I've been meaning to ask, do you think I need to hire protection for Josie and her family?"

I noticed he often avoided directly naming Tod, almost as if he wanted to deny the man's connection to the Pederson clan. That was maybe too harsh a judgment. I'd have to seek advice from my friend, Catherine. "Probably not, in answer to your question. So let me ask you the same thing

I'm asking everybody," I said. "Can you think of anyone in your organization, or with whom you associate, who would want Tod and Josie to stop looking for the crash site of your relative's aircraft out there in the Pacific Ocean?"

Pederson didn't hesitate. "No, I can't. And I've thought about it, ever since these incidents began to happen."

"It must have occurred to you that, if you withdrew your financial support, it's probable their project would collapse, and that would mean the burglaries and other incidents would stop. Why don't you just stop?"

Pederson looked out the window a moment and then said, "You don't have children, do you." It wasn't a question.

"No."

"If you did, you might not ask that question. I love my daughter. Even if she makes bad decisions occasionally, I can't deny her. Matter of fact, in some ways I hope she succeeds. Although she's never given me a full answer, I think this search has turned into an obsession for her. If she finally gets over it by finding the damn crash site, maybe some of the bad feelings in the family will be settled."

I raised an eyebrow. This was news to me. Sure, every family had issues of one sort or another, but he was alluding to something heavier and more persistent. Maybe. And maybe I'd have to follow up on that, too.

Pederson glanced at the clock again. "Mr. . . . Sean. I have a pressing appointment in a few minutes so . . ." He looked at me with a flat, non-judgmental expression.

I got his meaning. Instantly. "Thanks for your time. I'll get back to you when I have more questions," I said.

"I'm sure you will," he muttered under his breath as I stood and turned toward the door. It opened just as I reached it. I recognized the man who stood there. He was a lawyer with a prominent Minneapolis criminal defense firm. We nodded without speaking. He stepped aside as I exited and then went in and closed the door while I passed down the long well-carpeted hallway leading, I hoped, to the out of doors.

* * * *

GARY ANDERSON, whom I was led to believe was the principal personal attorney of Mr. Preston Pederson, was not a criminal defense lawyer, but a business law lawyer. So it wouldn't be unusual for Pederson to seek advice on criminal matters from a different attorney. That is, if he felt he needed such expertise. Did he? Maybe he'd assaulted someone. Pederson's nice tailored suits and quiet manners didn't fool me. The hand I'd shook that day in White Bear was hard and calloused and there was latent power in his arm. The other thing I mulled to no resolution while hieing myself to Minneapolis was that Pederson had seemed to be actively engaged in his daughter's search. I had thought Anderson's efforts to get me off the case had come at Pederson's direction. But now that I reexamined our conversation, I recalled that Anderson had never confirmed or denied that he was acting on behalf of Preston Pederson. But if not, who was he acting for?

An air horn suddenly blatting in my ear woke me to the fact that I was seriously tardy leaving a busy intersection when the light turned green.

CHAPTER 17

T OUR APARTMENT in Kenwood I heard a message from my honey telling me she'd only be a little late and to please thaw a steak from the freezer. "My carnivorous genes are raging, and I desire some beef and baked potato," she said in my ear.

So I found a nice thick T-bone that would do for both of us and selected the big spuds I would set to baking before Catherine arrived. She hadn't mentioned a salad but I knew her insistence on a frequency of greens was not disappearing. So I poked around our restaurant-sized refrigerator and located several kinds of lettuce, a reasonable-looking cucumber and a couple of 'shrooms.

I carefully thawed the steak in a plastic bag in a bowl of warm water to bring it to room temperature quickly. Then I built myself a lovely drink of thirty-year-old whiskey with a little ice and just a splash of water. I put the heavy cut-glass tumbler on the side table and flopped onto the couch. Staring at the ceiling, I took several healthy swigs and thought about my life. That meant I had to think about Catherine and our relationship, a pleasant enough task.

A few minutes later, I heard soft sounds in the kitchen and rolled over. I stumbled getting off the couch and when I came around the wall, there was Catherine in her sweats. She'd obviously been home for a while because an elaborate-looking salad was in a bowl on the counter and I could hear the snap and sizzle of beef searing in the broiler. I looked at my watch. Nearly an hour and a half had gone out of my life.

"Hi, sweetie," she said. "You were seriously out when I got home so I let you sleep. Rough day?"

"Not really, although my interview with Pres Pederson was odd."

"Tell me about it over steak. I'm focused on dinner right now and it's almost ready."

Catherine seemed at times to move faster than the speed of sound, multi-tasking, I think that's the word, with a vengeance. It was great. The steak was perfect, my spuds slathered in butter and sour cream, and Catherine's salad was the perfect side dish. With our inner needs satisfied we settled on the couch and I brought her up to speed on the case of Yap Island.

"I kind of thought at the beginning that it could be the father, that Pederson was trying to protect his daughter from the danger of a bad operation. But then that guy, Lewis, died. Murdered."

"Are you sure of that?" Catherine looked at me. "I know you told me the police in Winona are suspicious, but, as you sometimes say, where's the proof?"

I squinted up at her unlined face. "Yes, I do, sweet thing, and I also tell you, on occasion, that I sometimes go on instinct. On my gut."

"Not very elegant, but what does your gut tell you?"

"You really want to know? About my gut?"

"Well, actually, about your theory of the case."

"My gut tells me Mr. Lewis from St. Louis was murdered because he was bringing important information from his files to the Bartelmes. My gut says the efforts by Josie and her husband to locate the wreck of that bomber that killed her granduncle triggered some kind of ripples, like they tossed a stone into a pond. The ripples spread and people began to notice. I bet we'll find that Tod and Josie were being observed or tracked in some way from their first trip to the South Pacific. Then when they didn't find the wreck, I assume somebody figured that was it and they could relax. But Josie didn't let go of it."

"So somebody tried to discourage them with vandalism and theft."

"Yeah. Then enter an intrepid detective, yours truly. At about the same time, Tod found other veterans groups, started a website, and Stan Lewis got in touch with them."

"You think the plans for the trip this coming August was a trigger?"

"That and Stan Lewis deciding to take a train to Saint Paul."

"Why?"

"Ah, the big question, my love. Why? Why does anybody care if these folks find the wreck of an old bomber that went down back in 1944? I can understand why this has turned into a near obsession for Josie. It's family. A connection to her past. It's part of the same thing that brings folks to cemeteries on certain dates." I paused a moment. "There's only one reason that makes any sense to me."

I smiled at Catherine and took her hand. With her strong grip she helped me roll from flat on the carpet to a sitting, then standing position. She didn't relinquish my hand. Drawing it back against the rich curve of her hip, she pulled me closer. She pinched her eyes together and stared down at my face.

"And that is?"

"Something to do with the airplane Amundson was riding in."

"Will you go to the South Pacific?"

"Not hardly."

"Because?" She was still holding me close and fiddling with my ears.

"Because the case has come ashore here in landlocked Minnesota." I turned my head and stuck my tongue into her palm, tickling her.

Catherine's left hand dropped from my head and skated slowly down over my shoulder to my chest. She inserted two fingers between the buttons on my shirt and gently scratched.

"If you keep that up, I won't be able to remember everything."

"'S okay," she murmured, blowing in my ear. "Why do you think the answers are now here?"

We were sidling toward the bedroom, difficult to do when entwined as we were. "First, burglaries and theft of the Bartelmes' diving gear. Ouch. Then Stan Lewis. Then the shot at young Cal." By now her cotton sweatpants, loose around her waist to begin with, were sagging so I got a foot on them and held one leg to the floor. When she leaned away, they slipped almost to her knees, trapping her.

"Hey, no fair. You brought in reinforcements."

"I thought it was a clever ploy, myself." I shifted inside her arms and planted my lips on her now exposed breastbone. The move overbalanced us and we fell, chortling, onto the bed.

"That's it?"

"My reasons? Yep."

"What next, Sherlock?"

"Flush out the bad guy or guys."

"Not too original." We'd managed to extinguish some lights, lost most of our clothes and crawled fully into the massive bed.

"Wait 'til you hear my plan."

CHAPTER 18

I GOT TO MY OFFICE on Central late the next morning, still a little sore from the previous night's exercise. We'd talked about installing a small hot tub in the spare bedroom, but our research hadn't turned up anything that I thought wouldn't make the floor sag. So I'd detoured to my Roseville ranch and spent an hour soaking in the big redwood tank at the back of my house.

Now it was time to buckle down, so to speak. There were a dozen messages on my answering device. The last four, beginning at ten, were from Gareth Anderson, Attorney at Law. No message except to call him. Urgently requested.

Well, sure. I still hadn't told him I'd take him up on his offer to butt out of the Bartelmes' lives. When I had a client I just never reacted favorably to anyone except the client telling me to get lost. And even then, sometimes, I hung around. In this case I wasn't going to disappear, of course, especially now that some moke had taken a shot at my favorite teenager, Cal Pederson. How was he doing, I wondered? I called the Bartelme house. Maxine answered.

"Well, hi there, Boy Scout," she purred. "What can I do you for?"

"I was just calling to inquire about Cal. How's he doing?"

I repeated my request. Since I was unresponsive to her suggestive comment, she tried a different tack. "He's fine, will fully recover, I guess, and is back home in Chicago. His mom decided Josie wasn't taking good enough care of her kid."

I rang off, as they used to put it in those old English novels, and left the office after disposing of an accumulation of unwanted mail. I headed to the White Bear PD to talk with the investigator who had been assigned to the Cal Pederson shooting case. After I had located the likely place the shooter had stood and turned it over to the locals, the investigator in charge assured me they'd keep me up to speed on their progress. I went out of my way to try to stay on their good side. As with other aspects of this case, I hadn't heard anything about their progress, so off I went.

The captain of the homicide unit in White Bear Lake was cordial when I made it to his corner office. It was a nice if plainly furnished office with painted beige walls. The desk was large and piled with files. Unfortunately, Captain Nelson had little to tell me. "I understand your concern over the lack of much progress, Mr. Sean. But you know as well as I that this is a difficult case with almost no physical evidence."

"So what you're telling me is there's been no progress."

"Pretty much, except we've managed to eliminate almost everybody associated with the family as persons of interest."

"Almost."

"Yes. Alvin Pederson and his wife are out of the picture. So is the lawyer and both Bartelmes." Nelson shuffled papers in the file in front of him. "Pederson was at a construction site he's investing in. Let's see. We still have to verify Hillier's whereabouts and that of the other women buddies of Mrs. Bartelme. I think that's it." He closed the file, looked up and smiled. "No more brass in the grove of bushes you located for us, and no weapon. Any word from the Maplewood people about the break-in at the storage facility?"

I shook my head and got out of the chair. "I haven't talked to Tod today, but I've heard nothing. Thanks, Captain."

"Stay in touch."

I nodded and left the building. My plan was to head over to the Bartelmes and have another chat with Josie. I didn't get out of the PD parking lot. My rear tires were flat. Both of them. Unfortunately I didn't notice it until I nosed into the aisle so the Taurus was blocking part of the lot. I switched off, got out and trudged back to the reception desk

The woman handling receptionist duties looked a question at me.

"I need to call a tow truck. My car's in your lot with two flat tires," I said to her. "Is there a pay phone here?"

"No cell?" she inquired. I shook my head and she pointed to a phone on a nearby desk. "Dial eight to get an outside line."

I looked up a local garage and the fellow who answered my call said he'd be there in a few. I turned around and encountered a large man standing at the desk.

"Some dork parked in the aisle, blocking it," he said.

"I'm the dork," I said. "Flat tires. Tow truck is on its way. If you absolutely can't wait, I'll move it, but I hate to bust up my flats."

He looked down at me with what I took to be his long-suffering, disgusted look and turned away without a word. I went out to the lot again and waited in the sun for the tow truck to arrive. The driver was a young man who obviously knew his business. He maneuvered the truck until he could winch the Taurus onto the inclined flat bed and then drove us the four blocks to the garage.

Both lifts were full so I went across the street to a nearby bar and had a cup of coffee and a bad sandwich. When I wandered back to the service station, my automobile was on the rack with both wheels off and the owner waiting to give me an owl-eyed look.

"You got some enemies?" he inquired.

"Why?"

"Both tires got the same sickness. Look here." He showed me my wheels and pointed out a small, clean-edged tear in the tire right at the outside of the rim."One tire, maybe. If you hit something, a broken bottle, just right. But—"

"Aw, c'mon, Ron, you know that ain't it." The voice came from an old guy with a big belly sitting on a high stool in the office, clutching a can of soda. "That there is a knife cut, just like the other one."

Ron shrugged and said, "Yeah, that's probably right. Especially in two tires at the same time." He shifted and pointed at an almost identical cut in the other rear tire.

"Yeah," opined the old guy in the office. "Long time ago I wuz a dep'ty shrrif. Pine County." He interrupted himself to lift his close-cropped white head to take a swig of soda. His undersized shirt gapped between the buttons and he belched quietly when he lowered the can. "I still know a thing or two when I see it. Them two tires was slashed." Now he looked at me shrewdly. "You in some kinda trouble?"

I nodded and said, "Some kind, I guess. Put two new steel-belts on the wheels. Can you do that right away?"

Ron the service guy nodded and went to work. I whiled away the half-hour it took to replace my tires chatting with the ex-deputy. He had a few stories about a high-speed chase or two down the backroads of Pine County and seemed glad for the company. Just before Ron finished with my tires, the old man pulled a big railroad-type pocket watch out of his jeans and peered at it. Then he nodded as if satisfied with what he saw on the watch face. He rose, nodded to me and waved at Ron. Then without a word, he left the station and went slowly down the street.

The service guy manipulated the controls on the lift and dropped my Taurus back to the ground. Then I realized he hadn't used a pneumatic wrench to attach the wheels, but an old-fashioned tire wrench. I paid the bill with my plastic and thanked him for his prompt service. As I idled at the driveway onto Highway 61, watching for a break in traffic and waiting for the air conditioner to lower the temperature in the car, I thought about my two slashed tires. About the implications.

It was highly unlikely that targeting my tires had been a random act of vandalism. The car was in the police department parking lot, for God's sake. It wasn't a case of mistaken identity, either. Somebody was sending me a message. I wheeled onto the highway and headed toward my original destination, the Bartelmes' place on the lake. I only had the one case working at the moment, although I figured there was a remote possibility that a former thug I'd encountered was after me. I made a mental note to find out if anybody I'd helped put away was recently released from custody. Didn't seem a fruitful path of inquiry. Nope. This tire slashing was definitely tied to Yap.

CHAPTER 19

JOSIE MET ME at the door. It was immediately apparent she had been crying. Either that or she'd developed a sudden allergic reaction, and it wasn't ragweed season yet. I didn't comment other than to raise one eyebrow. "I need to talk with both of you. Is Tod here?"

I was pretty sure he was. I'd seen his car parked carelessly in the driveway. She nodded and waved me into the living room. The heat and humidity had become oppressive so the house had been closed up and the air conditioning cranked. Tod was sitting on the big couch in front of the dead fireplace, head in hands.

"There's been a development," I said without preamble. Ever the taciturn detective, that's me.

"I'll say," mumbled Tod. "I think we're screwed."

That wasn't the reaction I'd expected so I stopped where I was and looked first at Tod, then Josie. She walked around the couch and sank down beside her husband, taking one of his hands in her own.

"Maybe you better explain," I said, moving to a chair where I could see both Bartelmes and the entrance to the living room.

Tod heaved a mighty sigh and looked at me. "We just had a letter from our charter guy overseas. The first time we went to Yap, we went as tourists. While there we met some people who told us about this charter company in Singapore. They were able to get us a small salvage boat and industrial supplies we'd need to mount a serious search for the plane the second time we went over. So the first thing I did after we decided to make a trip this August was contact the company and reserve the boat and equipment we might need."

"We even put a deposit down," Josie said.

"And now?" I questioned.

"And now," she went on, "we get this letter saying they're sorry but there's been a misunderstanding and the boat isn't available."

"Not even if we change our dates," Tod said.

"Did you have a contract?" I asked.

"Sure, and we paid them a thousand bucks. They said they were sorry and the refund would arrive from their London bank in a few days. This really screws up our whole summer schedule."

"There's no chance of finding another boat to charter?"

Josie shook her head. "At short notice we might be able to get something else, but it'd cost a lot more. Money we don't have."

Tod lunged up off the couch. "We can sue for breach of contract, I suppose, damages or something like that," Josie said, watching her husband start to stalk around the room. "But that'll take ages and won't get us closer to the plane. Even if we win."

"Hang on a minute," I said. They both looked at me. "Can I see the letter?"

Josie went to fetch it. Tod eyed me and said, "What are you thinking?"

"Timing. Timing might be important. Don't they use email?"

"They do sort of," Josie said, "but for contractual things it's always been by regular mail." Josie handed me the letter, written on creamy heavy paper with an embossed crest of the commercial salvage company.

Taking the letter in hand, I said, "I came over here to tell you about an incident of my own. This morning I was at the White Bear Lake station house to find out if there's been any new developments about Cal's shooting."

"Have there?" Josie interrupted.

"No, but while I was in the building, somebody slashed the rear tires on my car. I take it as a warning that my involvement in this affair is creating some problems for somebody. Or potential problems," I amended.

"That's awful. We'll pay for the new tires, of course," Josie said.

"That's kind of you to offer, but that isn't the point and I won't bill you for them, anyway. In fact," now I was ad libbing, just making it up as I went along. I didn't want to use them like this but my sudden brainstorm would work better if I didn't have to rely on Josie and Tod's acting abilities. "In fact, you aren't going to get anymore bills from me at all, plus the original retainer, less a dollar for the old legal niceties, will be returned as soon as I can get back to the office and cut you a check."

Tod looked bewildered. Josie shook her head. I couldn't blame them for that. I was springing new deals on them as fast as I could make them up.

"I don't get it," Tod said. "You better explain."

"Try this. I've been contacted by parties who wish to remain anonymous but who are interested in your efforts to find your lost relative. The interests of this party are their own, and I wouldn't tell you even if I knew what they were. But I'll be able to bring you substantial financial help in a few days. Your trip to Yap may be delayed for a while, but not until next year, and not forever.

"Now, here's what you should do. Call a meeting, for, how about tomorrow evening or late in the afternoon? Invite everybody involved to come here. Tell your group you have an important announcement. When they get here you explain about this contract breach. Then you explain you've been working to locate a different charter company for a slightly later trip."

"But— Tod started to protest.

I cut him off. "Do that. Take the afternoon and make some calls. Negotiate another contract with the salvage people, if you can. Or at least, begin the process. And don't be quiet about it. We want the word to get around that you're going ahead in spite of this temporary setback. Call my office and leave a message as to the time for the meeting. I'll show up about fifteen minutes later. Then we'll explain."

"I don't get it," Tod said, "but I'll do it." His grin came and went.

"For one thing, you're going to upset somebody's applecart," I explained. "This letter is dated almost a week ago. My tires were slashed today. It tells me that if this foul-up is not legitimate, more than one person is trying to mess you up, and they aren't coordinating things. I gotta go. Trust me, we'll sort this all out fairly soon."

I left a quiet Bartelme living room and headed toward Minneapolis and the home of Madeline Pryor. I hoped she'd been sincere at the dance when she'd told me she was prepared to help in any substantial way she could. I was about to find out.

Chapter 20

THE PRYORS LIVED in an upscale part of Deephaven, a community on the southern shore of Lake Minnetonka, just west of Minneapolis. It took me twenty minutes to drive to the town and another ten on the winding lanes and multifarious cul-de-sacs and alleys to locate the address. I didn't call ahead. For all I knew, Mrs. Henry Pryor, Madeline, was at Cape Antibes or on the Cote d'Azure enjoying a holiday. But I didn't think so. The way she had talked to me at the country club dance led me to believe she was keeping close tabs on the state of the Bartelmes' south seas project.

I was keeping close tabs on my rearview mirror as I wandered about Deephaven. The efficiency with which my rear tires had been dispatched to the recycle bin during my short time in the PD building suggested I was being followed. I didn't see any obvious tail on the freeway to this western enclave, but there was enough traffic to make detection difficult, especially since I tend to watch where I'm going more than where I've been. Keeps me out of the wrecker's clutches.

Finally I found the right address and had myself buzzed through the gate. It, the gate, closed after me, which pleased me, since I doubted the tire slasher was on the premises. Mrs. Pryor, looking considerably less elegant than when I had last seen her, met me on the front steps.

"You're fortunate to find me at home. Do you always drop in without calling first? Let's go around to the patio. It's cooler."

"Thanks. I do usually call ahead. In this case, I just took a chance. Even if you hadn't been able to talk to me, it's a nice drive."

"I assume your presence here has something to do with the Bartelmes and their search for the missing plane?"

"That's right. I'm here today because I hope you were serious when you told me the other night that you willing to help Josie and Tod, should they need it."

"Oh, I was and still am absolutely serious. We like the Bartelmes. I admire her efforts to locate that plane wreck. My family has a military background, and the idea of not being able to locate the bodies of our deceased fighters is distressing. I have been a supporter of efforts to locate MIAs for years."

I explained to Madeline the foul-up over the Bartelmes' charter and the financial bind they now faced. I was beginning to suspect it was more of somebody's effort to scuttle the search. I still had to find out why in order to nab the skell messing things up.

After my explanation, we arrived at a sum that would cover my expenses and the inflated costs of finding a new charter salvage crew. Then we figured out how to conceal the source of the new funds.

"It would complicate the relationship between Josie and her employment if it becomes known I'm bankrolling her search. Do you see?"

"I do. We'll find an intermediary."

"I have a suggestion," she said. "I know of your friend, Catherine Mckerney, and her profession. She comes highly recommended. And I suspect the cash flow from her investments and her massage therapy school and contracts will make it possible to launder a contribution. Is that the right word for what we're doing?" She smiled.

I was getting the impression she was enjoying herself. "Yes, that would work. You can make out the check to her, and I'll deliver it. Then she'll write a check for the identical amount to the Bartelmes."

We finished our iced teas and I left with a check for $26,000 in my hand. *Nice doing business with you, Mrs. Pryor.* I wondered if she was even going to tell her husband about our transaction. Well, that was her business. Mine was to help salvage the Bartelmes' search and trap the scoundrel who was killing people and dropping mines in their path. I did register the fact that Mrs. Pryor had some prior knowledge of the kind of under-the-table financial dealing we had engaged. Yes, I now believed there was some kind of conspiracy at work, a conspiracy dedicated to keeping the Bartelmes away from their granduncle's downed bomber.

Back in my slightly overheated office, I examined my mail and decided to catch up on some other business.

I went to my file of due and overdue bills and to my checkbook. Paperwork was not my favorite part of the business, but vital. I tended to require cash or check payments up front to cover daily expenses. I learned early on that even apparently upright citizens could renege on agreed payments to the detective after the fact.

Not long ago I'd had a fairly tense conversation with a client. I'd been hired to locate the possible hiding place of a series of packages. It seemed a small manufacturing firm was experiencing a surprisingly high number of delivery losses. Their plant would manufacture the gizmos, in this case some sort of complicated electrical switch, and then package the order. The order would be inventoried and go to the truck for delivery. Delivery truck guys would load a hundred packages of switches. A day later the gizmo purchaser would report the delivery short by five or ten items. Apologies and adjustments would follow.

There were always such occasional adjustments, my client had said. But he was noticing a disturbing increase in the frequency of such claims, and, therefore, some loss in profits. He hired me to do some surveillance and to try to locate a thief, if indeed there was one.

I did and there was. Now the client was balking at the final payment. I knew there was something odd about the set-up when I showed the client the digital tape of the culprit. I'd recently converted from a still camera to a small hand-held digital video camera for jobs like this one. But I didn't carry a laptop. I brought a disk.

"So this is a copy of the original?" he asked, all the while staring intently at the screen.

"Yep. The original is in my safe." I didn't explain that my safe wasn't much, but I used phrases like that to calm concerned clients who might be afraid of revealing something unintended. Or embarrassing.

"Do you recognize the guy?" I pointed at the screen where the culprit was off-loading some cartons of the missing gizmos. Culprit was male. I knew from the way he moved but I was too far away to ID the guy and why would I risk it? I wouldn't know him, right?

"Okay," the client sighed. "I've seen enough."

"Here's the address of that storage unit," I said, "and my final bill."

That was more than a month ago and I still hadn't received a check. Usually I tried to get final payment at the time I deliver the final report. I don't remember exactly why I hadn't in this case.

Today I knew why. When I checked back to the storage unit location, I discovered—and videotaped—just what I'd expected. Client and culprit were there together, piling the gizmos into a panel truck from the storage unit. I recorded more video.

When I later showed the video to Catherine and we studied the movements of the two men, it was obvious they knew each other and that the client was pissed at the culprit.

"I bet the smaller one is a relative. You think?"

"Exactly my thought," I smiled. "Let's send a letter—no, better, let's email my client that I'll be forced to take my evidence and my case to his company board if I don't get a payment ASAP." So we did that.

CHAPTER 21

I WENT TO MY OFFICE, parking around the corner instead of in the lot where I regularly put the car. I figured whoever the dork was who'd cut my tires, he knew my vehicle and he'd find it all right, but if I parked on the busy street instead of in the quiet lot, he was less likely to take a chance and tamper with it.

Because it took a few minutes longer to reach my office, I wasn't there to get the phone call from Josie. One might think that was a significant event, my missing that call, because, if I had, I would have realized . . . and so on. I find phrases like that in what I call my training manuals, that is, my detective novels. Wilkie Collins did that sometimes. Pregnant phrases or pauses. Sorry, it wasn't like that. This time I'd remembered to leave my answering machine on so I could listen to the message.

There were four messages. Two were from a lawyer in Eden Prairie who wanted me to find a former client, somebody named Darrel who had taken it on the lam and left a large bill for services rendered. Another call was from my honey, who was packing to drive to Rochester for some business meetings. She'd be gone overnight. Wow. I was footloose and so forth tonight. The last message was from Josie, telling me the family and some of the investors were gathering for a war council to make decisions after this latest disruption.

I dialed home. It was important I talk to Catherine before she left town. She didn't yet know I was about to use her as a laundry service to protect the identity of a new investor. Fortunately, she was still home.

"Hey, Sean, glad you caught me. I'm within inches of trotting out the door."

"Me, too, and I know you're in a rush to get going, but I have a big favor to ask. If you weren't about to leave, I'd beat it home to talk with you, because this is something I'd prefer to do face to face."

"Whoa. Sounds ominous. It is legal?"

"Yes, but it involves a lot of money. Your money." I went on to explain my plan and the circumstances that led up to it. "So I really need a check to take with me tonight."

"You want it on my personal or my business account?"

"Personal, I think. That way if there's a hassle, the school and your contracts won't be involved."

"Good thinking. How much did you say? $26,000? I can handle that, but I'll have to make a transfer while I'm in Rochester. So the Bartelmes shouldn't rush off and cash it tonight."

I knew that wouldn't be a problem. They didn't need cash right now, and I planned to lay the check on them well after the banks closed this evening.

"Okay." She came back to the phone. "I've left the check on the table by the phone. See you don't spend it all at once. Oh, and here's an idea. Get a promissory note. The lawyer will be there, right? Anderson? He can write it with you as my agent. Some kind of easy terms. You know, like low or no interest for some long term. That'll make the whole thing appear more legit."

"Good idea. And I'll make this check from Mrs. Pryor over to you and deposit it in your bank when I come pick up your check. Have a good trip. I'll figure out a way to thank you later."

We made kissy sounds at the telephone, and I sat back to plot out my next few hours. This was going to be an interesting meeting this evening. I hoped all the principals would be there.

* * * *

I ROLLED INTO the driveway and parked beside a dark-green Lincoln I recognized as Preston Pederson's ride. I briefly considered where I might put the Taurus midst several highly polished newer vehicles. But hiding it was not an option. Its faded, unwashed blue exterior stood out like a used digit.

I pressed the doorbell and unlatched the gate. Tod met me at the door to the house, and we went on through to the veranda where this whole business had started. The entire cast was present, plus the other two Js, Jennifer and Julie. I got a few sketchy waves but no smiles. Apparently they'd already had some of the bad news.

"Sorry to be late," I murmured, sitting in a chair on Tod's left so I could see the faces of the people there.

Josie nodded at me and continued. "Anyway, the killing of Mr. Lewis—" I thought her voice wobbled a bit there "—and the loss of whatever information he might have been bringing us, and all these other things that have happened, have put a real crimp in our plans for the trip to Yap this summer. I'm just not sure what we can do except delay the search until we can save some more money. Tod and I have talked about it, and we don't feel right asking you to put up more money for this obsession of mine. You've already been so generous and understanding."

I glanced around at the faces. They all looked pretty solemn.

"One of the things we can do to economize is terminate Mr. Sean, here," Preston said. "I was never in favor of hiring him in the first place."

I stood up. Looked around. Smiled. "That's your choice, of course, but I don't think you're going to be ready to dismiss me after you hear what I have to say."

Making speeches wasn't one of my strengths, but over the years I'd learned a thing or two about the dramatic moment, the build-up and then the fist in the gut, so to speak. "It's true I can't pin down the party responsible for these problems you've been having. Yet. I'm sure I'm getting closer to answers."

"How do you know that?" said Hillier.

"Somebody slashed two of my tires. Whoever it was took a big chance and did it while I was at the police department in White Bear." There were murmurs. "I think I'm being warned off because I'm getting too close to answers.

"We now know Stan Lewis was not only murdered but was robbed. It's very likely he was bringing some files of papers here, records and other materials he'd developed over the years having to do with the activities of men in the bomber wing. You see, Lewis apparently thought some of the boys in the group were doing a little business on the side. You've probably all heard about the drug running that happened during Vietnam, right?"

Gary Anderson stood up and stretched. "Excuse me." He smiled around the group. "This is beginning to sound like a long session. I wonder if I could have some more iced tea?"

"I can get you something stronger," Tod said.

"Iced tea's fine."

After everybody settled again, I went on. "The smuggling business didn't originate with World War Two. The government conducted a fairly extensive investigation after the war. They were looking into charges and evidence of smuggling drugs, money, and jewelry aboard military transportation."

"I don't think I ever heard anything about that," Pederson said.

"You were probably too young, and the government didn't do any publicity on it. There were very few prosecutions. But then came Stan Lewis. Apparently he decided he should have been cut in to whatever deals were happening out in the South Pacific, or maybe he thought they shouldn't have happened at all. We'll probably never know. What I do know, and so do the cops in Winona and St. Louis, is that Stan Lewis was murdered and the briefcase he was carrying was lifted. What's more, several files pertaining to the men and missions of the bomber group he was assigned to on Los Negros that Stan developed are now also missing."

Was I stretching things a little? You could say that. More like stretching close to the breaking point. That's okay. Cops lie, so why can't a PI have a little flexibility?

"But, that's not what I came here to say." Always leave 'em wanting a little more, right?

"An individual with whom I'm closely acquainted has stepped forward and expressed interest in this project. I have here a check."

Tod leaned toward me and plucked the paper from my finger. He whistled.

"Wow! Twenty-six thousand. This will give us enough to replace the lost gear and hire a new charter boat."

Josie and some others began to make appropriate noises, and Maxine grinned and applauded quietly. Jennifer stood up and did a little victory dance and whistled through the attractive gap in her front teeth. I watched all of them, trying not to be too obvious about it. After a little hesitation Josie's dad stood up and ceremoniously shook my hand. He didn't look what I'd call enthused. Neither did Anderson or Hillier.

After the celebration died down, Preston said quietly, "I suppose this means we're going to have to put up with your investigation a while longer."

"I suppose so," I responded. "I sort of feel obligated to keep an eye on my lady's investment."

"You must have had a time convincing this Catherine Mckerney to put up twenny-six g's," smirked Alvin.

"Not really," I said."She trusts my judgment on many things."

"Mckerney, Mckerney," Gary Anderson said."Why is that name familiar?" He took the check and peered at Catherine's signature.

"Maybe because she's a board member of a small bank your firm represents," I said. "First Meridian in Robbinsdale?"

Anderson looked blank for a moment and then shrugged. "I take it this is why you haven't returned my calls."

I nodded. "That's a logical conclusion."

Josie looked at us. It was apparent she was picking up some undercurrents between Anderson and myself. That was all right. Without revealing the questions I had about Anderson's agenda in this congregation, I wanted Josie and Tod to be more cautious around all these people because somebody here, I was convinced, was responsible for their troubles. I still didn't know why, or who, but I would find out. Oh, yes. And if there was to be blood in the street, I was going to make sure it wasn't mine or my clients. About the others, I wasn't so certain.

CHAPTER 22

I T WAS GETTING LATE and even though there was still sunlight in the western sky, traffic was light, so I had time to think. I had the windows open because it was a nice evening. Interesting how the odors change as one drives through a city. Apart from the stink of diesel and gasoline exhausts, I felt and noticed the smell of the river as I crossed the Mississippi. The damp gave way to curry and then barbeque with a whiff of mesquite. The corner that held an Arby's gave me a shot of hot frying oil. Trees and green and damp arrived as I rolled into Kenwood and slid the car into my spot in the underground parking garage.

Upstairs, the apartment felt empty. It was. Catherine had left for her business trip. The fact I knew she was out of town somehow made the empty apartment feel different than if she was just out somewhere in the city. I should have stayed at home in Roseville. But I built a drink of scotch and a little ice, then settled down for more noodling about my clients and their troubles.

Josie's college buddies had joined the effort to find the downed plane wherever it lay under the Pacific Ocean. I didn't quite get it. Family support I could understand. The loss of a brother or uncle in a war with the resulting empty grave made for unhappiness. Families often wanted their military dead in a military cemetery, like the local one at Fort Snelling, so their support was logical. But why these two women, neither of whom seemed to have a lot of money to throw around, contributed several times to Josie's campaign wasn't so clear. Maybe it was just the romance of the idea. Maybe there was something else there, something under the surface. Maybe I'd better find out.

I went to the third and smallest bedroom, where Catherine had her office and the computer setup. Not long after we'd become a couple, after it had become clear we were going to be involved with each other, maybe for life, Catherine had set up her computer so I had access to most programs. I didn't use modern technology much, preferring an eyeball-to-eyeball, hands on approach. Blackberries were for eating, preferably with thick cream and sugar. Dessert. Cell phones were mostly, in my view, a way to avoid human interaction. Nobody I had ever encountered in this life needed to be connected twenty-four seven. Gives one an inflated and erroneous sense of self.

But there were times when the Internet could be helpful. For most stuff, I had my connection with the Revulons. Here in Kenwood, Catherine occasionally helped or, as now, I helped myself. I held subscriptions to a couple of professional data search operations.

I booted up, logged on and found my notepad and pen. First up, Julie Alcott. A stay-at-home mom, she'd told me. Two youngsters, one of each, in the local public schools. Married, Julie's husband worked in Stillwater for a realtor. Not a licensed salesman or broker, he was in the back office. More treading tappity-tap over the keyboard. Waiting. *Ah, here we are.* The screen filled. The Alcotts owned their own home and had for several years, had registered a boat, and appeared to have never been in trouble with the law. There was a reference to some sort of college dustup in the nineties. But they had no outstanding warrants in the state of Minnesota, no court judgments, no recorded driving violations.

For an additional fee, a deeper search. No thanks. I entered Jennifer Martin's name. Her husband, Terrance, I learned earlier, was the owner of a chain of dry cleaning stores in the northern and western suburbs of Minneapolis. The Better Business Bureau informed me there had been the occasional complaints, all handled with dispatch. Their rating was satisfactory, and they were regular contributors to a variety of civic and other causes, including the Republican party of Minnesota. Then I found a birth certificate for an Enid Marie Martin. The record indicated the girl was born to Jennifer and Terrance at the address in White Bear.

I checked my notes and couldn't find any reference to children. I searched further and discovered a death certificate for a girl child of three years with the same name and address. Cause of death was not indicated. That was unusual, but clerical errors did happen, and it didn't seem to be relevant. Again, a message appeared suggesting more information was available if only I'd pony up some more money. Again, I declined.

I traveled elsewhere along the humming wires and silicone and satellite connections until I discovered Terrance Martin had borrowed heavily to finance the establishment of his cleaning chain. What's more, the loans had been privately placed, meaning no bank was involved. That was a wall that could be breached, but did I need to make the effort?

I decided to leave that for another time. It was getting late. I had a small nightcap of some mighty fine Cointreau and went to bed.

* * * *

IN THE MORNING I called Mrs. Pryor to thank her for her help and briefly explained I had been successful in covering up the true source of the money. I don't usually keep clients up to the minute on my investigations, but this was a special sort of situation. Besides, she wasn't really a client, although I assured her I'd tell her the outcome whenever the case was finally resolved.

Catherine would be back this evening, I was happy to remind myself. When the phone rang, I answered it instead of letting it roll over to the answering machine. It was the Winona cop who had the Stan Lewis homicide.

"I just thought you'd want to know, the ME has wrapped up his examination, and we're gonna bury Mr. Lewis this afternoon in the local cemetery."

He's a vet, right?" I said.

"Yeah, and his remains will be moved to a federal site after they get through with the paperwork."

"I'll drive down," I said. He gave me the time of the ceremony and directions to the city cemetery.

Several hours later, I stood beside a large man in the dress uniform of a captain in the Winona Police Department on a still, sun-swept slope in one corner of a Winona cemetery. Across the freshly dug grave at rigid attention ranged a four-person honor guard of veterans. They stood holding flags that drooped in the heat and absence of moving air. I was sweating, even though I wasn't exerting myself in the slightest. A minister of some denomination in a black suit with a high white collar stood at one end of the casket. There was no one else there to see this veteran of that enormous conflict called World War Two placed in a temporary grave. Stan Lewis, Air Force gunner, late of St. Louis, Missouri, served his country honorably and then lived an apparently quiet life thereafter for more than sixty years. He died violently in a town he probably had never heard of, on a train beside the water of a river that flowed all the way to his hometown.

I decided that, even though I didn't know the man, he ought to have some justice in this world, and it looked like it was up to me to find it for him. He probably wouldn't thank me for the trouble I'd take, but there you go. We do or don't do things for many different reasons, some of which make little or no sense to others. I didn't care.

I was going to find whoever it was who fired the bullet into Stan Lewis and then dumped his body on the train tracks in Winona.

* * * *

IT WAS LATE when I got home, after stopping at my office to check the mail and messages. That didn't take long. There was only one recorded message and the mail was all crap. I thought about the message—from a lawyer I knew only slightly. I might not even recognize him if we chanced to meet on the street. He was a junior associate in a very large law firm for which I did some work a few years ago. He'd been designated as my contact at the firm. I had led him to believe he could be helpful in future work if he kept in touch.

So, he started calling me occasionally. Meaning maybe every couple of months. I had originally expected I'd have more frequent additional assignments from the firm, but it hadn't worked out, so there was not much he could provide. But he called anyway. And now this.

I almost didn't recognize his voice on the tape. He didn't leave his name but did leave enough information so I figured it out. What he told me was that word was going around I was becoming unreliable as an investigator. He didn't tell me the source, but I figured it out for myself. Attorney at Law Gareth Anderson was starting to turn the thumbscrews. He wanted me gone from the Bartelmes' problem in the worst way, and he wasn't above trying to mess with my rep and thus my business.

Pissing me off could be a dangerous pastime. For one thing, I was good at what I did and most attorneys in the Cities who knew about me were aware of my record. So his effort to dirty me probably wouldn't do much damage unless I let it go on for a while. Second, Lawyer Anderson's efforts made me wonder about him. Maybe he had something to hide. I would make it my business to find that out.

CHAPTER 23

FINDING SOME DIRT about Attorney Anderson took less time and effort than I expected. For one thing, I was good at my job. Did I mention that? Being good at my job meant I had a steady traffic in cases of various kinds and so had a number of contacts in multiple levels of society. Some were not individuals you'd want to meet in a dark alley off Hennepin Avenue, even if the city has reconstituted a formerly seedy block.

First I made a few calls to learn a little more about Lawyer Anderson and his friends. I found out where he lived—in a nice medium-sized mansion just off Lake of the Isles. Actually, it wasn't far from Catherine's and my place. Then I sent one of my construction pals around. He backed his big dump truck up over the curb onto the Anderson's soft boulevard lawn, making a few ruts in the lawn. When he went to the door he sort of leaned on Mrs. Anderson, not physically, you understand, but pushing the misunderstanding. Turned out to be the wrong address. I was never sure whether she had the presence of mind to take the truck's license number, but it wouldn't have mattered. The truck was being moved to Wisconsin, and the license plate was seriously covered with muddy tape. The truck left the scene, but the ruts remained.

The next morning, Anderson's secretary reported she'd received a vaguely menacing phone call before he got to the office. That same morning, somebody had banged a vehicle into their trash receptacle before the company truck had arrived. The Andersons' front lawn was quite a mess.

Later in the day, Anderson himself got a call at his office and heard only some heavy breathing. It went on long enough Anderson got rattled and hung up the phone with a bang in my ear. When he left the office that day, he was probably startled, driving out of the underground parking ramp, to encounter me just standing there beside the ramp entrance, looking at him. At least, that's the way it seemed. But I didn't even turn my head as he went by although I made sure to make eye contact. No smiles, no little head nods or a tip of the old fedora. He drove away. I didn't look after him. Why would I? That way he'd be sure I was there. Or maybe not. He'd think about me. And wonder why I was standing there outside his building ramp just at that time. Then he'd think about the ruts on his pristine lawn, the call to his secretary, the heavy breather.

I'd wait just a day to see if he got the message. This all might seem petty, even juvenile, but it was relatively harmless. I could engage a more formal legal process, amass sufficient information to sue the bastard, but that would take time and money. The time lost could be dangerous to my clients.

While the pranksters were at large, I was learning more about the Bartelmes and about Josie's father, Preston Pederson.

I decided I should go back to the East Side retirement home to talk with Abe and Tommy some more about their ex-boss and those good ol' times. I called the home and talked with Abe, who said he'd round up Tommy and be ready when I got there. An hour later I pulled into the driveway of the place to find Abe sitting alone on a bench outside the main door. He looked even gloomier than his sagging jowls usually indicated.

"What's up, Abe? Where's your buddy?"

Abe shook his head. "Tommy ain't here. He had a heart attack, I guess, or mebby a stroke. Ambulance just left."

I touched the old man's shoulder. "Gee, Abe, I'm sorry to hear that. Do you want to go to the hospital? Where'd they take him?"

"Regions. I sure would like to go. Tommy's the only family we got left. Each other, y' know? But we ain't kin, so they wouldn't let me see him."

"You let me worry about that. C'mon. I'll drive you there and see you get back here okay."

I helped him into the front seat and we sped off to Regions Hospital. It wasn't far. While Tommy settled in a chair in the Emergency waiting area, I went looking for a friend of a friend, a nursing supervisor in another part of the hospital. Like all these places, she knew people and about half an hour later, a nurse I didn't know came to where we were sitting.

"Are you Sean Sean?"

I allowed I was that person.

"Your friend is in the ICU. You can go up to the floor and ask for Ms. Jordan. Use my name if you need to."

"Thank you," I said.

We elevatored up and entered the hushed environment of the ICU. Ms. Jordan had been clued in and escorted us to a closed room. "You can go in, but I'm afraid your friend's been medicated, so he's not likely to be awake."

I gestured Abe through the door and watched. Abe approached the bed slowly and gazed down at his friend. He reached out a gnarled hand and gently slid his palm under Tommy's where it lay on the sheet. I went to find myself a cup of coffee. When I returned, I found Abe just leaving Tommy's room, and a doctor and nurse standing by the bed.

"They wanted me to leave while they examine him."

"How is Tommy doing?"

Abe shrugged. "He's got tubes and things in him and he's just lyin' there, like he's asleep. An' I guess he is."

We sat together in a small lounge. Abe slumped forward, legs spread and hands clasped between his knees.

"We knew our times would come, but it's hard. We're all the family we got, you know? Outlived 'em all. I hoped I'd be the one to go first." He glanced over at me. "Selfish, huh?"

I shrugged. "You feel up to talking to me about Pederson's old man?"

"Sure. What do you want to know?"

"Tell you the truth, I'm not sure."

"Just fishing, huh?"

"Something like that," I said. "Tell me more about when you first went to work for Pederson's father."

Abe nodded and rubbed his forehead. "I can't remember exactly when I started. Tommy was already there. It must have been around 1950, probably a year or so earlier. We were just kids. Missed the draft 'cause the war ended. Big Jack had a project. He was building near the old Payne Reliever, that strip joint? Anyway, I was looking for work that summer so I just went on down, and there was Tommy. I remembered he'd told me he had landed a job there. Tom sort of talked Big Jack into hiring me part time. That's the summer I met Kid Cann." Abe glanced sideways at me as if to see my reaction.

"Kid Cann?"

"You don't know who he is, do you?

"I guess not," I said.

"That wasn't his real name. People said he was a gangster, a mob guy."

I raised that practiced eyebrow. It was supposed to take the place of asking a question. Sometimes it worked.

"His name was Isidor something. He was a tough kid who grew up on the North Side of Minneapolis. A lotta Jews lived up there in those years."

"A ghetto?"

Abe just looked at me like he didn't know what the word meant. Maybe he didn't.

"Anyway, he got into a lotta stuff and some people said he'd killed a couple of guys back in the thirties or something like that."

"Did he get arrested?" If he'd been in a courtroom there'd be a record somewhere. Did I care?

"I guess. I heard he went to jail eventually, then moved to Florida. He's dead now."

"Abe," I said, "what does this have to do with the price of anything?"

"Here's the thing. After that first time when Kid Cann came to the construction site, he never came back but another guy did. Every week or so. Some guy who looked like a crook. He was a big guy who didn't look comfortable in a suit, you know what I mean? He'd show up and him and the old man, Pederson, would go into the construction shack for few minutes. Then the guy would walk out and leave. He never said nothin' to any of the rest of us. I remember he always had a shiny new car. One time it was a Studebaker. Did you ever see one? One year they looked the same, front and back. My dad said you never knew if it was comin' or goin'." He grinned.

We talked some more and it became clear to me Preston's father was making regular payments to somebody for something. I couldn't think of another reason for the guy in the suit showing up so routinely. I had no proof, of course. Of anything. It could have been protection, or it could have been to pay a loan, or it could have been blackmail. All it did was make me realize Pop Pederson wasn't a stranger to the seamier side of life in the big city. So it wouldn't surprise me if Josie's dad was somehow involved in whatever this was.

The problem I had was that Josie's dad was in no way estranged from his daughter. In my observations of the two of them as well as in conversations with others, it was clear they had affection and love for each other. The entire family was pretty close, even if Dad was getting a little tired of supporting his daughter's efforts to locate their long-lost relative. Love or not, though, I expected Dad wasn't about to let his daughter expose some illegal past activities that could get Dad sent off to prison. Maybe he'd decided to torpedo the effort and things had gotten out of hand?

More questions. Not many answers. I could see Abe was focusing more on his buddy Tommy, so I wound it down. I made him take some money for a cab home when he was done at the hospital. I left Abe waiting for Tommy to regain consciousness and drove home. I wanted to reexamine the cast of characters and see if I couldn't whittle it down to manageable size before someone else got killed or maimed.

Chapter 24

THE FARTHER I GOT into the case, the more convinced I was that somebody in Josie's family or somebody closely allied with a family member was involved. Either that or something about the quest for Uncle Richard had opened a dank vault somewhere, and the zombie that crawled out was following a smudged trail of footprints in the wet sand.

First, it was fairly obvious the shooting of Cal was either a mistake, as in an unfortunate case of wrong place and wrong time, or the shooter was really, really good. Killing the boy, I reasoned, would bring down a flood of law, not just the lonely PI presently engaged. So if I could leave that alone, hoping the forensics would turn over the right rock, I had the family of both Josie and Tod, none of whom seemed likely to have the contacts or the resources to want to discourage the quest. With two exceptions I knew of.

One was Josie's dad, ol' Pres Pederson hisself. The other was Hillier. Although he worked for Pederson, he could have his own separate agenda. I would check him out further.

My first *mano a mano* encounter with Mr. R.P. Hillier hadn't gone particularly well, although I'd learned a few things about his present situation. He was probably a partner or a heavy investor in Pederson Enterprises. His role was what was politely called a facilitator in some circles. In these circles, if there was some small bloodletting or doors to be kicked in, intimidation and threat making, he was the man to call. I presumed he had a small stable of thugs he could call on, maybe even at one or two removes.

My first efforts were remote. I did a wide area Internet search for my target, Mr. Hillier. While the bits and bytes were trembling and assembling, I used the old-fashioned telephone to make a call. With a code word that changed frequently, I was able to obtain a different telephone number. I had to do that three times before I got a street address. To that address I mailed a short query, the name, Social Security number, current address, employment, and a couple other pertinent details. I did not sign the paper. Nor did I put a return address on the envelope.

Unless the paper was found and examined by some forensic genius, and why would it be, there was almost no way to trace it. I could have worn latex gloves, but that was going a bit far. I knew the letter would be burned after the information was digested. It was an interesting sidelight, I think, to know in this high-tech surveillance era, one way to avoid detection was to use low-tech, old-fashioned means of communication, like the U.S. mail and landline telephones. Not fast, mind you, but almost undetectable.

I mentioned the advantages of low-tech communication to some-body in a bar once. We were having a drink and talking politics, I think. My companion said, "What about phone taps? And you know the feds some-times open your mail, right? And they can get a cover to record incoming and outgoing mail addresses, right?"

"Look," I said. "Why would they tap your phone? And you can go find a public phone somewhere, like in a library, or a filling station."

"I suppose."

"And if you don't want your letter intercepted, go mail it across town, or across the river and use a phony return address. There are still intercepts at NSA from World War Two that haven't been translated. I think surveil-lance people in the FBI and other agencies are drowning in information."

I was reading an old manual about old weapons when the door hinges whined. They were an early warning signal if someone tried to ease my office door open and surprise me. The door was never locked when I was in residence. Why bother? Most people knocked and I hollered "come in" and they did. If the door was locked I had to get up, cross the office and open it, and that put me face to face with whomever. I'd rather be at my desk across the space, ready to dive for cover. Or a weapon.

Anyway, I looked up and She entered. She was put together the way I would have done it, before CM. She paused in the doorway to give me time for a good gander. I looked in her eyes, then dropped my gaze to the floor. I scanned slowly upward from her feet, propped up by lethal-looking four-inch heels, trim ankles, nicely swelling calves and hips, right on up past an impressive bosom— and I've seen some—to broad, capable-looking shoulders. My analysis hesitated at her mane of gloriously blonde hair that hung about her face like a crowd of jealous suitors. Whatever she was wearing—I didn't know what to call it—hung on her awesome body like a seamless piece of plastic cling wrap. No cleavage, a high neckline on the pale blue wrap that matched the color of her eyes. She was taller than I was. But then, most people were.

This vision of feminine beauty paused, slightly hip-shot in my doorway. I judged her a Four B: Big, Beautiful, Blonde and Blatant. "Good morning," I said, pleasantly. "How may I help you?"

Her smile seemed to add light to the room—bright, straight white teeth framed by luscious-looking red lips. She straightened and followed her breasts into my office. "Have a chair," I gallantly indicated my favorite and most comfortable side chair. For just a moment I regretted it was bolted to the floor.

She nodded. In a plain-vanilla no-nonsense tone of voice she said, "Good morning, Mr. Sean. My business with you is confidential, sensitive, and worrisome to my family and my associates. So if you don't mind, I have a few questions before we get into intimate detail."

I didn't mind. Of course I didn't mind. I wasn't so taken with her beauty I failed to assess the possible firepower secreted in her small handbag she held in her lap. She crossed her knees and decorously tugged the tight skirt down a little.

"My name is Lorelei Jones." She stopped as if to give me a chance to respond. I remained politely silent and attentive. Lorelei Jones inhaled with a rustle of fabric and went on. "We've—I've investigated you, and I'm satisfied you're discreet and can handle my case."

I nodded and with my right hand moused to the X in the right-hand corner. My computer screen went blank. "Were you recommended to me? Or did you find me in the Yellow Pages?"

She smiled a slow smile, full of obscure possibilities. "You aren't in the Yellow Pages, Mr. Sean, at least not the ones I consulted."

Points for her.

"Here's my problem, Mr. Sean. My mother is deceased, and my father is living alone after almost forty years of being married. He's a retired surgeon and he's bored, I think. He lives very comfortably in Wayzata. He seems to have taken up with a woman. A much younger woman."

"This younger woman is likely to be less comfortable financially than your father. Am I correct?" I smiled. Lorelei inhaled. It was distracting, but not blatantly so. Warning bells sounding in my head upon her appearance were tolling more faintly. Maybe this was legit. Lorelei Jones couldn't help being a sexpot, could she?

"Yes. I can't say for sure she's a gold digger. You understand. But my father does have a lot of money, and I just want to be sure she isn't taking advantage of him." Lorelei pouted prettily. "I don't need his money. It isn't that. I just . . ." she gestured vaguely as her voice trailed off.

"All right. I can look into this." I quoted my rates and the necessity of an advance.

Lorelei wrote out a check and recited some particulars I noted on a pad on my desk. We stood up to take leave of each other. At least, I stood up. Lorelei rose from her chair in a kind of undulating motion that reminded me a little of a stripper I once knew, or maybe Venus in a clam shell. We touched fingers, and she smiled, again lighting up the room and my life. Because her dress was so thin and so tight, the lower part had ridden up, requiring her to make some adjustments as she went out. She didn't tug so much as she seemed to caress the fabric down over her hips and over her fanny.

I was entranced.

I sank back into my chair. My hand automatically went to a lower drawer where my digital Nikon with the long zoom lens nestled. There were two vantage points, one window at the rear overlooking the parking lot, the other the street in front. Lorelei Jones didn't seem to me to be a parking lot kind of woman. I went down the hall and readied the camera. Moments later my new client appeared on the sidewalk, and I was able to snap several pictures of her swaying to a late model BMW parked at the curb. I was rarely wrong about such quick judgments of people.

Just like in the movies. People like that woman always seemed to find the most convenient parking places. Although the angle was high, I knew the close-ups when she opened the driver's side door would give me an identification, should I need one from another source. Like the cops.

CHAPTER 25

I REPAIRED TO MY OFFICE again after checking to be sure the photographs were adequate for the job. Then I booted up the old computer to see what bits and bytes had accumulated since my oh-so-pleasant interruption by Ms. Lorelei Jones. She wore no wedding ring, and I thought she either had a dynamite hairdresser or her shining blonde locks were natural.

There wasn't a lot of new information to be had about Mr. R.P. Hillier. Even less lent itself to my investigation. He had no police record, a clean service record, and an honorable discharge. Unmarried, he'd apparently lived in the Twin Cities for a good number of years. He was employed by Pederson and had been for a long time.

I had managed to fiddle out some financial information which only confirmed something I suspected in the first place. Pederson Associates was a private financial service and investment house, so it didn't file public stockholder reports. It did, however, have to meet certain governmental requirements. If you knew where and how to enquire, and I did, you could winkle out bits and pieces. One of those bits was that Hillier was on the board of directors of Pederson and Associates, as was that attorney, Gary Anderson.

The telephone rang. Madeline Pryor. She wanted to talk to me in person. Could I come right over? I could and would. Hillier would have to wait. I was sure he wouldn't mind.

When I arrived forty-five minutes later, Mrs. Pryor her very own self opened the door. Her welcoming smile was somewhat less than enthusiastic.

We went through the house to a sunroom at the back. The room had a fine view of well-cared-for lawn. No lake. After a few stiff pleasantries and a cup of strong, nicely brewed coffee, we got down to business.

Pause. Gentle sigh. A turn of her head and a level gaze into my eyes. "You have the gift of patience, haven't you?"

"Thank you. I find that waiting quietly usually results in a more forthcoming result."

"I've asked you here, Mr. Sean, for a couple of reasons. I—my husband has made inquiries and believe you to be honorable and discreet." She smiled a little and nodded. "Such old-fashioned words, but important concepts in a polite society. I think we've lost a good deal of that through the years of technological advancement. Don't you agree?"

I didn't say anything. I recognized that Mrs. Pryor was gearing up for some revelatory conversation. I didn't want to interrupt her concentration.

"My husband doesn't entirely agree with my telling you some things, but that's his training. Lawyers and accountants seem to be programmed to reveal as little as possible about everything. Hmmm. I asked you here to talk about diamonds. More specifically, about my diamond necklace, the one you admired the other night at the club."

Mrs. Pryor leaned to her left and slid open the drawer of a small table beside her. She took out a flat leather box with a padded cover. It was a jewelry case, black, soft, and expensive looking. The box probably cost as much as the diamond earrings I'd given Catherine last Christmas. She set the box on the table between us and opened the top. There it was, her diamond-and-ruby necklace in all its magnificence. And it was all of that. I leaned over and admired it. Then I looked at her. She watched me with an intense gaze.

"I wouldn't know if this was the same stone you were wearing the other night. I also wouldn't have the foggiest if this is a fake of some kind."

Mrs. Pryor nodded as if I'd reacted correctly or passed some kind of secret test. She smiled. "It is, and it isn't paste. There were others."

"Others?"

"Yes, a—um—a relative brought them to me. Well, to my father, actually. He was in the Pacific Theater during World War Two. I think he was a spy, but I'm not really sure."

She smiled again. I thought she was beginning to enjoy herself. "The family story goes like this. Before and during the war, our government was anxious to place a number of covert agents in key positions in the Far East. I had several relatives who had spent extensive time around the end of the nineteenth century in China and in the Far East pursuing business interests. They made themselves available to our government. When the war ended, some of them stayed in the Far East. They continued to take advantage of business opportunities and contacts they had developed. The government was anxious to get the service boys home as soon as possible, and they weren't too worried about security. Apparently there was a fair amount of smuggling." She smiled.

"For that matter, there was a good deal of smuggling *during* the war," I said softly.

We both looked up as a young woman, possibly a maid, entered with a coffee service. Apparently she thought Mrs. Pryor and I were sucking down a lot of coffee. "Although it may surprise you to know it, I have some awareness of the ways of the wealthy in some of these matters," I said.

The young woman was casually dressed and properly deferential. She set down the coffee pot and picked up the one we had been using. Mrs. Pryor poured me another cup of hot, strong coffee and then continued her story.

"It was apparent to many of these servicemen, and a few women, I believe, who were given the opportunity, that bringing home uncut jewels was easier and safer than carrying drugs or actual cash."

I nodded and sipped. Or sipped and nodded. "So what you're suggesting is that the history, or shall we say, the provenance of this necklace is unknown."

"Correct, Mr. Sean. We know from whom the necklace came, and when, but its history prior to 1946 is a mystery. My husband and I have become aware over the years that a number of our friends and family members have acquired and sold such gems and jewelry."

"Do I surmise that you're wondering if that may be the source of the current difficulties our friends the Bartelmes are having?"

"Suppose their uncle, Mr. Amundson, was carrying gems the day the aircraft was shot down? Either for himself or as a courier for others. And suppose those others now don't wish that fact to be revealed."

I sipped again and smiled at her. Since she was thinking along lines similar to my own, I decided to confide a bit. "All right. Let's just suppose, although we have absolutely no proof of this, that this fellow Amundson, either on his own or working with others, was carrying a valuable stash of jewels. Let's further assume he may have acquired these jewels through, shall we say, extra-legal means. Let's also assume he didn't plan to pay duty or declare the gems when he entered these United States. And let's suppose he was carrying some kind of records to indicate who paid, or who was to be paid. That is, to whom the jewels were to be distributed. The details of the transactions don't matter much at this point, just that there was a record. Not that there's much of a chance that the record might surface, but somebody here's worried. Worried enough to try to sabotage Tod and Josie's expedition. Worried enough to kill poor Stan Lewis."

Mrs. Pryor sipped, but she didn't nod. "My thinking also," she said. "I cannot believe Tod or Josie had anything to do with that man's murder, but if her father did, he must be exposed."

I finished my coffee. "I'm still not clear why we're having this conversation," I said. That wasn't true, but I wanted her to say it out loud. Implied intents were all right in romance novels, but in my world, we needed plain talk.

"I asked you here, frankly, to make my own judgment of your character." She looked me in the eyes. A forthright woman, Mrs. Pryor. Being mostly forthright myself, I stared right back. "I suspect the Bartelmes may need some financial help and you may also need additional resources. I'll require an accounting, but you may come to me for additional funds if that is necessary. Please understand, whatever the outcome, my involvement should remain private. But I assure you, Mr. Sean, whatever additional resources you need to put this matter to rest so Tod and Josie may complete their research will be available."

She gazed at me, having completed her pronouncement. I had the feeling this was a speech she had been preparing, but wasn't quite ready to deliver when I showed up on her front door. I didn't believe for an instant tat she or her husband were in any way involved in the present crimes I was investigating. Other than paying for my investigation indirectly through her support of Josie and Tod's quest. But there were surely lingering questions that might, one day, rise again.

We were both standing now and moving toward the door. Mrs. Pryor rested one hand on my forearm as if to maintain an important connection. She had told me what I expected to hear, but she hadn't gone the whole way. Making the saboteur go away was one thing. Nailing the killer of Stan Lewis and Preston Pederson might be quite another.

CHAPTER 26

AFTER I DIALED 911, I called detective Simon in Minneapolis. Since the guy was dead on my office floor, it was the correct thing to do. I knew when the call went to the Minneapolis homicide unit, Simon would have to excuse himself from the case because of our long-standing and well-known friendship. That was to be expected, but I gave him a heads-up so we would both have some inside tracking if needed.

While I waited the few minutes for the cops to arrive, I checked Josie's dad's body. He was dressed in sandals and what looked like upscale swimming trunks. Except for the bloody hole in his bare chest, he could have been asleep. In fact, he looked more peaceful than I'd seen him in a long time. I was tempted to frisk the body but I forbore, because the cops were going to have a field day when they discovered my extensive involvement with the prominent developer.

I sat at my desk and listened to the sirens draw closer. Why sirens, I wondered? I'd told the dispatcher the guy was dead, and that I'd had first aid training so I knew the signs. Maybe the units were having a boring shift and this was a little excitement. I decided not to call Josie or her husband. The authorities could make the notification while I tried to figure out my next move.

I was leaning heavily on the premise that her dad, Preston, was the man behind the efforts to torpedo Tod and Josie's efforts to find her granduncle's plane off Yap Island. I was further convinced his empire had been built on the sandy foundation of stolen gems, which he'd used as collateral for his investment and construction empire in the Twin Cities. But now he was dead, and not by his own hand. This raised the possibility that a manipulator lurked behind the curtain, someone who also stood to lose big time if the smuggling activity was revealed.

Two young uniformed officers filled the doorway to my office. They glanced at me and at the body. One of them sidled carefully around Pederson and came to my desk. He fished out a notebook and began to ask me questions.

Ten minutes later, an investigator also unknown to me appeared in my door and the routine began again, now in deadly earnest.

* * * *

IT WAS NEARLY 10:00 P.M. when I was finally released and allowed to go home to Kenwood. The body would, in time, be released. The Bartelmes and others had been notified, and I had assured an agitated Tod Bartelme I would be able to see them at their White Bear home around two the next day.

And so it was that I approached their place on a warm sunny afternoon, noting as I walked across the parking apron that I recognized some of the vehicles. It appeared the whole family was gathered. Birds sang joyously and I thought it was too bad. No one should be weighted with the sadness of abruptly planning their father's funeral, no matter how much of a criminal he may have been, and that was still an open question.

Inside, the atmosphere was muted. All the usual suspects were present, and the bar was open. The questions came swiftly and my answers were unsatisfactory. I explained over and over again that I'd found Mr. Pederson when I got to my office the middle of the previous day. The police were doing their thing, and I had no idea to put forth as to who might have wanted him dead. That was a lie, of course.

Since he had been such a dominant figure, for a time no one seemed in charge. Josie sat mostly mute, a handkerchief clutched in her fingers. Tears occasionally tracked down her cheeks, and she stared out the window at the lake. Tod paced and asked questions to which either he knew the answers or there weren't any.

Eventually, exhaustion leaked into the room and the silences became longer. Shadows began to crawl across the floor. The lawyer, Anderson, made a few efforts to take the lead in getting organized. The question of my investigation arose more than once. Anderson wanted to terminate my involvement. Tod and other members of the family, principally Maxine, demurred and requested I remain involved.

"I don't understand your reasoning," Anderson snapped at Tod.

"I do," said Maxine. "It's pretty obvious Pres's death is connected to these trips to Yap Island."

Anderson shook his head. "I don't think so. I don't see any evidence of that."

Maxine shrugged and accepted another highball from a woman I hadn't met. "Well, this is another incident in all this stuff that's been happening since Josie and Tod decided to try to find Uncle Richard's plane. How can it not be connected? I don't mean to make light of his murder, but we have to realize we're all involved, everybody in this room," she waved the hand not holding her glass. "What if some lunatic is after all of us? I sure as hell want him locked up before somebody else gets hurt." Her voice became shrill and she took a healthy slug of her drink. I noticed her hand shook, just a little.

"I do see some links," I interposed. "All of the trouble, including the wounding of Cal, the break-ins, and the murders of Stan Lewis and your father, Josie, are linked. It must somehow be connected to your efforts to locate the B-24 bomber that took your granduncle to his death."

"I think you're reaching for feathers," growled Anderson. "You just want keep the fees coming. Meanwhile, you can't seem to point to any progress in solving the break-ins. I think you ought to be terminated." There was a tiny pause, as if everybody recognized his unfortunate choice of words.

"Stop this," said Tod. "This is our decision. Josie and I will deal with all this after the—after the funeral." Josie rose abruptly from the sofa and left the room with her head bowed. She didn't make eye contact and kept a white handkerchief pressed against her mouth. The door closed softly behind her.

"As your attorney," Anderson went on, "I think I'm in a position to give you some important advice." His voice had sharpened. Why was he pressing so?

"Mr. Anderson," Tod said," You are—*were* Mr. Pederson's attorney, not mine. We may want to retain your services, but please don't make assumptions. We're grateful for your support up to now. All of you. But we are not going to decide much of anything today except funeral arrangements. Mr. Sean, can you give us any idea when the body will be released?"

I watched Anderson decide to subside for the time being. He sat beside the newcomer, his wife, I assumed. She took his elbow in a familiar way.

As I left the Bartelmes' home and the grieving family enmeshed in shock and wonderment at the brutal and sudden ending of the life of their patriarch, the threats had become more real and closer. The thickening night air warned of rain. I had become more than a little intrigued by Lawyer Anderson's attitude. He was clearly anxious to have me removed from the scene as soon as possible. As I reached my car it became one of those Minnesota nights. Soft rain fell, the streetlights making orange glows above the wet, glistening streets. It was the kind of rain, with temperature in the low eighties, that makes you want to take off all your clothes and stand naked, face uplifted to the dark sky, until all your sins and missteps are washed away. When the chill sets in, you go inside to a hot bath and somebody's loving arms. I intended to drive home to Roseville, but just outside the Bartelmes' driveway, I decided to do something else, and, to this day, I can't say what impelled me to stop, pull off on the verge and adjust my rearview mirrors so I had a clear view of the driveway forty feet behind me. Fifteen minutes of waiting and I watched Lawyer Anderson and his wife get in their car and exit the parking area. I made a discreet U-turn and followed.

We wandered at a sedate pace down through town until we hit Interstate 94. Anderson turned west, and I followed. I assumed he was finally heading home. I stayed two or three cars behind the black Caddy the whole way through Saint Paul. Occasionally I could see Anderson and his wife, or at least their profiles, as we swished through the night. Then he began to pick up the pace to match traffic.

I was in a tight snake of vehicles, tracking through the night, following the flickering red taillights ahead. Two vehicles behind me gave it a closed-in feeling. Anderson's was the third car ahead. We were roaring down the freeway, sliding across lanes and zipping right down a narrow ribbon of macadam onto another freeway, this one northbound. The rise and fall of the road and the snake we were in, the rhythm of almost synchronized swaying and adjusting speed, the flashing of brake lights, reminded me of watching conga lines of drafting long-distance skaters. We were cocooned in our steel-and-aluminum rockets. Radios and engines isolated each driver, if they were anything like me.

I topped the hill and we dipped down the narrow access to junction with 280, the highway that headed north toward my house. I caught a small flash of light under the rear of the third car ahead. It was just a momentary flash and not very bright. It was about the size of a small backfire from a muscle car shifting down, or a low-rider bottoming out briefly on the pavement. But then everything went to hell.

At first it was like a movie. In slow motion. For a few long seconds, our line continued down the grade, but as we cleared the abutment on the right, the car I was tailing, the black Caddy, drifted right and began to fishtail. It suddenly wrenched out of line, crossed two lanes and rammed head-on into the bridge support. It hadn't slowed at all. Our conga line scattered like a flock of birds, fishtailing and skidding over the entire junction. We were fortunate there was no other traffic that rainy night. I headed up the shoulder, hugging the left side, almost scraping the barrier fence, and stopped thirty yards on. In my rearview mirror a large bloom of red and yellow light from the Caddy filled the space under the bridge. There was no way anyone could have survived.

I wasn't sure what to do at that moment. If I stayed, my investigation might be irretrievably compromised. The asshole in the car, the guy I was following, might have led me to whoever was pulling strings. Flashing blue and red lights were blossoming all around me. I put the Taurus into gear and slowly drove up the glistening highway while the windshield washers cleared away the gentle summer rain.

The next day I called the Minnesota Highway Patrol.

CHAPTER 27

MY INTERVIEW with the patrol reps was neither pleasant nor nasty. I resisted the sergeant's attempts to weasel out of me my connection with the dead attorney and/or his wife. If I had thought it would make a difference to their investigation of the fatal crash, I would have gladly owned up to it.

"But you were acquainted with the deceased, correct?"

"Yes, as I told you, Mr. Anderson is an attorney. He represents Preston Pederson and some or all of his various enterprises. That's how I knew him. We had no direct business dealings."

"And this Preston Pederson is now deceased, correct?"

"That's right."

"Pederson was found dead of a gunshot in your office, correct?"

I sighed. "Look, I get you want a clear record in this interview, but I've already told you all that. I have no idea why Pederson was in my office when I wasn't there. Did he break in? I don't leave my door open when I'm out. You need to check with the Minneapolis PD for their progress on that case."

"Rest assured, Mr. Sean, we will."

"Can I leave now?" Since I wasn't under arrest, and in fact, had readily agreed to this interview at patrol headquarters in Saint Paul, I knew I could just walk out, but I didn't want to unnecessarily antagonize anybody. "Or, can I ask a question? I saw the accident. Is there something unusual about it? Anything?"

The patrol officer smiled slightly. "Mr. Sean. I checked you out and you come with good credentials. So I'm going to level with you."

Yeah, right, I thought. He leaned forward slightly.

"This wasn't an accident. There's evidence that an explosion resulted in Mr. Anderson losing control of his vehicle." The sergeant continued to stare into my eyes. I met him, blink for blink.

"Really. So the flash of light I told you about was some sort of explosion? Do you have any ideas about who would have wanted to murder Mr. Anderson?"

The man across the table flinched ever so slightly. I'd just preempted his next question. We stared at each other for a moment in silence. Then he relaxed and said, "We're only in the preliminary phases of this investigation. I'd appreciate it greatly if you'd keep us informed of any new information that might bear on our work. Thank you for coming in."

He stood up. So did I and we left the room without shaking hands. I departed the building and went to my car. The meter had expired and there was a parking ticket on the windshield. I shoved the ticket into the glove box—if they still call 'em that—and drove to my office.

The door was open and three uniformed crime scene techs and a detective investigator were there. The investigator, whom I didn't recognize, checked my ID and told me pleasantly they'd be out of my way and out of my office in just another hour, so why didn't I go get lunch and a cuppa joe. I talked the guy into letting me listen to my telephone messages, which didn't provide me with anything useful. The building manager had left two requests that I stop in at my earliest convenience.

I went downstairs and talked to George. He didn't much care what I was involved in, he was just filling in the blanks on the company forms. We had a casual chat, and I went up the street for a ham sandwich and a small dish of slaw. When I got back to the building the door was shut but not latched and the police were gone, leaving a surprisingly unrumpled office. The biggest problem was the left-behind fingerprint powder residue. It made me sneeze.

I pulled my paper file on the diamond business and reviewed the list of players. It was shorter now with the death of Lawyer Anderson. I decided I'd better have some background beyond what I already knew about him. I ambled down the hall to my favorite duo, Betsy and Belinda Revulon. With their hacking skills, I knew they'd plow the ground about Anderson and reveal to me any dirt to be had.

"I assume this is more trackless effort, yes?" asked Betsy when we'd dispensed with welcoming hugs. After all, we hadn't seen each other in all of two days.

"Correct." Since the two murders closely connected with the Bartelmes' efforts to locate Josie's granduncle, I was becoming wary. More than usual. I hadn't begun to flinch or dive for cover at unexpected noises but there was something going on that I wasn't seeing. "I think I better take you two to dinner soon, or pay you a fee."

Both women smiled down at me and waved me out the door. It occurred to me that escorting these two blonde Valkyries to dinner at a nice downtown restaurant some crowded evening would enhance my standing around town, if not my stature. Something to think about.

Late in the afternoon, Betsy Revulon showed up empty-handed.

"Nothing?" I asked.

"Not nothing, but nothing substantive. Actually, what isn't there is the most intriguing part of the picture."

"Enlighten me."

Betsy slid into my guest chair and frowned when she couldn't move it. "Mr. Gary Anderson has a clean bill from the day he entered law school. William Mitchell, to be precise. A slow, unspectacular rise to associate in that big law firm in Saint Paul. Then in 2001, he joined four other lawyers here in Minneapolis to form a firm of their own. They do a variety of labor, family, small business and corporate law. The partners have supported various political candidates, generally to the right of center."

"I'm not hearing any eyebrow-raising facts."

"Every so often, six times over the past thirty years, to be precise, Mr. Anderson's work load at his law firm has dipped. It's like he just disappeared for a period of time."

"Poof," I said.

"Poof," Betsy agreed. "My first thought was he went off on a pilgrimage or some volunteer experience for a church or nongovernmental organization. You know, like the groups working in Haiti or Africa. Can't find anything. He's off the radar. Sometimes for weeks, once for six months."

"Rehab of some kind?"

She nodded. "That's one possibility, but we can't say for sure one way or the other." She rose from the chair and sauntered to the door. "Do you want us to make further inquiries?"

I shook my head. "You covered thirty-plus years. I guess that's enough. Wait. When was the first time?"

Betsy glanced at a scrap of paper in her hand and said, "Summer before he started law school, 1983." She went out with a little flip of her fingers.

"Wait," I called.

Betsy's blonde head reappeared. "You summoned?"

"I have another thought. Here's another player to check out." I scribbled Richard Hillier's name on a yellow pad and handed the torn out sheet to her.

Betsy took the paper, kissed the air over my head and disappeared.

CHAPTER 28

I WAS IN EARLY the next morning organizing my notes and discovered that nobody had called my answering machine overnight. I was questioning motives, everybody's. For some time I'd been leaning toward Preston Pederson as the killer. His abrupt death by gunshot was a certain clue there were other yet undiscovered dimensions. And I still had no idea why Pederson's corpse had been so oddly dressed. According to the family, the last time anyone had seen him alive was early the morning he was shot, and he'd been dressed in a swimsuit, raggedy old t-shirt, sandals, and carrying a beach towel. According to Maxine, who supplied the description, he'd been walking across the deck, heading in the direction of the beach. Since that had been just after dawn, and I found the corpse at about nine, there was only a three-hour gap. Who filled it with animosity and death?

What about Tod or Josie? Since they had instigated my involvement and appeared to be intent on pursuing their search for Amundson's bomber in the sea off Yap Island, I had to assume they were innocent. I could conceive of no rational reason why they would persistently try to sabotage their own expeditions.

Jennifer and Julie, Josie's girl buddies, had no reason I could discover to be involved in any of this. Nor did I seriously consider the other Pederson family members—Alvin, Maxine, or the boy, Calvin. It wasn't just the fact that Calvin had been wounded on the beach. What sixteen-year-old boy would have a deadly stake in seventy-year-old events on the other side of the world?

Stan Lewis, the murdered World War Two vet from St. Louis, was out of the picture. His connection was much closer, even than any of the local family. And then there were the others, Lawyer Gary Anderson, Richard Hillier, Lorelei Jones, even Josie Preston's dead father.

In my mind there was a conspiracy here. It had begun during the waning months of World War Two, in the Pacific Theater, and I thought it somehow had to do with thefts, smuggling, and the acquisition of wealth and influence through illegal means.

A soft rap on my doorframe brought me back to the present. Belinda Revulon's shining face and luxuriant head of honey-colored hair captured my view and my attention.

"You have something for me?"

"I do, honey. I do," she husked.

"Come. Sit. Tell." So she did.

"Here is a timeline on your target, Mr. Richard Hillier. Thirty years ago, give or take, the boy was living in Gary, Indiana. His family was unremarkable, upper blue-collar. Later, he attended a college in northern Illinois, went to work in Des Moines and then to Omaha to a construction company and in 1995, moved to our fair cities, where he hooked up with Pederson Construction and Development."

"Any signs of malfeasance?"

Belinda smiled. "Wait. Let me call your attention to a timeline we produced earlier. Like yesterday."

"What? Who? Oh, sure."

She laid a piece of paper in front of me. Both Revulons had a taste for the dramatic. I recognized the name at the top and smiled at her.

"Just so. Mr. Hillier's timeline triggered our memories, so we did some crosschecking with your earlier target, Gary Anderson."

I could tell she had something juicy. "So, tell." I leaned back in my chair and smiled.

"It seems Mr. Anderson and Mr. Hillier are long-time buddies. They went to the same high school in Gary, Indiana. Anderson was a year behind Hillier in school but they played on the same football teams.

"Later, they attended the same college. Then Mr. Anderson went to law school and Mr. Hillier went to work. For a construction company in Des Moines, as I said earlier." She smiled again. "That's in Iowa."

"Yes, it is."

"The Des Moines company is owned by the same people who own the Omaha company that later employed Mr. Anderson."

"Is that a fact."

"It is, and what is also interesting is that both have family connections to an investment company in Chicago."

"My, how the web entangles."

"Oh, there's more," Belinda said. "On two occasions, almost identical dates, mind you, both Mr. Anderson and Mr. Hillier went off the grid for short periods of time, like a week. We can find no evidence of resignations or of either being temporarily laid off or any reason for their disappearances. But it's clear in our minds, Betsy's and mine, that those two have long been on closely joined paths and they went somewhere together for something."

"But we have little or no concrete evidence of that."

"Unfortunately, that's true. However, neither Betsy nor I have the slightest doubt you will take these facts and our conclusions and make something wonderful out of it all."

"Wonderful, I doubt," I said. "I'm more inclined to see collusion and crime here. Thank you, so much. I am, as always, in your debt."

Belinda departed and I contemplated my next move, based on this new information. My first assumption was that Anderson and Hillier were up to something. Something that was illegal and of long standing. It did occur to me that maybe they were off on a fishing trip somewhere. I had to check it out. Fishing? Possibly, but I'd bet it was something tied to the construction trades in three states but now centered in the money game here in Minnesota. I needed more information so I sauntered down the hall and lodged yet another request.

"There are three companies in the construction business linked to all this," I said to Belinda after thanking her again for their efforts on my behalf. "I believe I need additional background on each of them. History, ownership, like that. And, if you please, I want to know about their support of the war effort."

"Specifically, I bet you mean the Second World War."

"Yes. Further, it would be interesting to discover if anybody tied to the companies during those years was in military service and—"

"And did any of them serve in the Pacific Theater, yes?" Belinda had a sometimes annoying habit of finishing my sentences. Sometimes.

"Exactly."

She nodded enthusiastically, understanding just where we might be going. I left the Revulons to their tasks.

I wondered if we'd discover the Pryor name in our searches. I hoped not. I liked Mrs. Pryor, and she'd helped, both with financial support for Tod and Josie and by raising the specter of the jewel smuggling activity.

I made a series of summary notes in my computer and logged off. It was time to head home to Kenwood. More and more, I realized, I was thinking of Catherine's apartment as home. That was a good thing.

CHAPTER 29

S OUNDS AS IF YOUR CASE is becoming more instead of less complicated."
Catherine's voice floated from the kitchen to the living room, where
I was relaxing on our couch with a little Scotch and the early evening
news on TV. I hit the mute button. The news wasn't that interesting, anyway.
Riley Sparz was talking about dogs in hot cars or something.

"You'd think it would begin to sort itself out, people being murdered
and all."

Catherine had become sort of used to my mordant humor, but I was
careful not to disparage those on the wrong side of the law, even the dead ones.
She continued to believe there was some good in all of us, even those ripping
off NGOs trying to help the less fortunate among the world's populations. "I
had the sense you were leaning toward Josie's father as the head saboteur."

"Right you are. Even though that was disturbing, he just seemed to
be right for it. And he has, or had, these questionable associations."

"Dinner is served in our elegant kitchen. Bring your drink. What
associations?"

So I enumerated Pederson's associations. While I did so, it occurred to
me, not for the first time, that a good deal of his clout in the local construction
business had come about because of his father's connections, particularly the
political ones. I made a mental note to pursue the politics further.

"What is it about the death of the lawyer, Anderson, that bothers
you so much?"

"Apart from the fact that he was murdered by a bomb in his car and
that his wife, who was probably innocent of any involvement, died with him?"

"Apart from that."

"These *au gratin* potatoes are spectacular," I said.

"Thank you. How do you like the pork tenderloin?"

"Also spectacular."

"Do you know why Anderson's death bothers you so much?" Catherine asked again, eying me over the thin rim of her wine glass.

"I don't think I am muchly bothered. At least, not any more muchly than usual."

"Yes, you are. And it's because you were there. What? Four or five car lengths behind him? And you saw the flash from the bomb. And you saw the crash."

"Honey, I've been closely involved in killings before, some by my own hand."

"I know that. And in the past, as now, each of them has disturbed you. In this instance, I think you're wondering if your presence might have triggered the event. I think you're wondering if somebody who was also observing Mr. Anderson may have seen you trailing the Andersons, and that made whoever it is decide they couldn't wait. He had to be killed to keep you from finding out something important."

I stared at the ceramic tile under my plate and traced the lines of the joints. I didn't go in much for second guessing or introspection. Most PIs didn't, I suspected. We did what we did and moved on. Our efforts at mental gymnastics were mostly reserved for trying to outguess the adversary or determine our next moves. Catherine's insights were a little disturbing. I could already tell she was right on the money. I'd have to be a little more careful about unburdening myself in the future.

Catherine put her hand over my restless finger. "I think you're feeling a little direct responsibility. If your following Mr. Anderson hadn't happened, maybe his wife would still be alive."

I looked up into her concerned face. I could understand she was at least partially right. "Yeah, if that's why he was killed, my presence may have been the motivator."

The next morning Catherine whisked off to her massage school while I cleaned up the kitchen and the rest of the place. Then it was time to spend some serious effort fleshing out Anderson's background and his connection with Richard Hillier.

Anderson's law firm was located in a small, obscure strip mall on the border between Edina and Minneapolis. I parked in one of their client/visitor spots and confronted the receptionist. "I'm sorry to bother you today. I know it must be hard, having just lost one of the partners, but if I'm to prevent any more damage to your employers, I need to see a senior partner right away." It was mostly bullshit, of course, but I was counting on the turmoil surrounding the murder and my ominous statement to break through their normal shields.

The woman opened her mouth to say something negative, I had no doubt, when a big burly man dressed in a very expensive dark suit crashed out of an inner office and came striding down the short hallway, bellowing, "God damn it! Somebody has got to have the key to that asshole's desk." He caught sight of me and without the slightest hitch in his stride, transferred his frustration to my small self. "And just who the hell are you?"

Now, I could have been a prospective client, about to bring his firm a million dollars worth of business, and at that minute, he could not have been less interested. He stormed up to the edge of the reception desk and stuck his face down to mine.

"Well?"

"Mr. Larson, my name is Sean. I must speak with you about your re-cently murdered partner, Gareth Anderson."

"Gary? What's your connection with this mess?" He drew a quick breath and swung his large head toward the woman, now standing at her desk. "Ruthie? Go through that box of stuff again. Anderson's keys must be in there. Now, you. What did you say your name was?"

"Sean Sean. I'm a private investigator."

The man had his mouth open, no doubt to send me out the door. I could almost see my name register in his consciousness. There's a certain level of satisfaction when that happens to a short guy.

"Sean Sean. Oh. Yeah. I found your name in Gary's stuff. Just now. In his date book."

"He didn't have a smartphone or whatever?"

Larson started to turn away, then glanced back. "Backup," he said tersely, not explaining. "You'd better come with me."

I followed lawyer Larson to a corner office, past a couple of closed doors with no nameplates. His office wasn't very large, with a single tall, narrow window that looked out on a sun-washed parking lot. Apart from a single framed diploma, the light yellow walls were empty of any decoration. Larson's desktop, a big wooden one, was cluttered with files.

"Sit," he said. He didn't have to tell me which chair, as there was only one besides his desk chair. He was a big man and his throne reflected that.

After I alit, he contemplated me for a long moment. Finally he exhaled and said, "Gary's death has been a huge blow. He was handling a bunch of cases, several of which are coming to resolution soon. It's gonna be a bitch to get up to speed, and I hate continuances."

"I'm really only interested in one client," I said. That was a lie, of course. Had Anderson not been murdered, I probably wouldn't have cared about his other clients, but, as they say, that was then, this is now. "Mr. Anderson was the attorney for Preston Pederson. I'd appreciate anything you can give me."

"Well, there's still client-attorney privilege attached, you know. He handled Preston's business for many years, did most of the family's wills, some labor contracts, an occasional vendor dispute, all the usual for the kind of business Pederson was in."

I nodded and started to ask the same question in a different way when Larson interrupted.

"I have two entries in Gary's appointment book with your name attached. That's why I recognized you. We're trying to reach out to all Gary's contacts and clients. If you can tell me why you consulted him, I'm sure we can help." This guy was bulling ahead, attorney reticence be damned. I needed to play for a little more time.

"What were those dates again?" I asked. He gave me the dates, both being in the immediate past when we'd been at the Bartelmes. Then he stared at me, fingers squeezing the edges of the date book. "Nothing earlier?" Sidney Larson shook his head. So I had been right. He hadn't wanted his partners to know about our lunch meeting, the one where Anderson had tried to get me to back off and abandon Tod and Josie. In another office, a clock chimed.

"What about taxes, corporate or personal? Did Anderson involve himself there?"

"No." Larson shook his head. "We have a tax firm that takes care of this partnership and several of our clients. Anderson had no involvement with IRS law, far as I know, and I knew Gary pretty well."

"Besides the construction business, I understood he was getting pretty active recently in the markets. Was that part of Anderson's portfolio?"

"I can't say for sure." Larson spread his big hands over the desktop. "I presume it was although we haven't researched all the files yet. You understand."

I nodded, but did I? "Socialize much? You know, parties with families, the occasional lunch or dinner with clients?"

"Some. Oh, sure, we all know each other's families to a degree, but mostly that was separate. Anderson didn't have any children, thank God, and he seemed to prefer the company of Preston Pederson and some of his financial cronies."

"Was Richard Hillier one of those cronies?"

"They went to school together, you know. So, maybe if you tell me what you're looking for, I could help more." Larson leaned forward and shuffled some of the papers under his fingertips.

"Contacts, Mr. Larson. Associations, networks. Background work is what I do. Putting meat on the bare bones."

"Yes, I suppose so. And what happens to the meat you dig up?"

The images were getting a little gritty. I shrugged.

Larson shifted in his chair. "Well, it was a tragic accident. I can't understand how it happened." He scratched his nose. "Look, I'm very interested in what's going on, so I'll put together a list after we get into Gary's desk. I'll shoot you a copy of whatever I think's relevant. You can take it from there. Depending on, there might be a small retainer attached."

As I stood to leave, I spread my hands in the universal sign of ignorance. We shook and I left, smiling to the receptionist. *I might need to see her again. Accident, Larson had said. Didn't he know Anderson and his wife had been murdered? Or was he trying to probe my knowledge?* I wasn't happy with Larson's control of the information he was going to release, but I sensed if I pushed, he'd get his back up and I'd get even less. Sometimes you just go with the flow, but I had to wonder if Larson was being as open and straight with me as he appeared. Maybe that was his technique: appear easy, even eager, while in reality just letting out the bare minimum. Well, we would see.

CHAPTER 30

THE PURPOSE OF THIS INQUIRY is to determine whether there is sufficient cause to hold defendant over for trial," the judge said. "I would
remind everyone to avoid wasting the court's time with rambling and
irrelevant commentary. Let's, in the vernacular of the times, cut to the chase."

The judge sat back and rapped his gavel. I didn't know what the case
was, nor did I care. I had tracked Investigator Ricardo Simon to this courtroom to suggest we meet for lunch as soon as he was released.

I slid out of the pew and out the door to pace restlessly in the corridor. It wasn't that I was under any real time or other pressure. I just wanted
to get on with things. In due course, the attorneys, prosecutorial and de-
fender "cut to the judge's chase" and the doors opened to expel the people
from the courtroom, my detective friend among them.

"Let's go over to the French Café," Ricardo said as he took my arm.
"I'm in the mood for some French onion soup."

He was always in the mood for their onion soup. "How's tricks?" he
said once we were seated at a small table in the corner.

"Tricks are sort of normal. My trick today has to do with the death
of that attorney, Gareth Anderson and his wife."

"Oh, yeah, I heard something about that just this morning. There's
some jurisdictional dustup. It's not my case."

Our soup arrived and he dug through the thick cheese covering, letting a burst of fragrant steam emerge. "That's what I want to ask about. I was
interviewed by the state guys yesterday, but it seemed to be a pretty light-
fingered approach, when I thought about it."

"It happened in Ramsey County, you know, so we're not involved."

"I know it did. I was there when it happened."

Ricardo raised his eyebrows and took a slurp of hot soup. "I didn't
know that."

Since it appeared I was privy to more current intel than he was, I explained that Anderson and his wife had been murdered by means of an explosive device planted somewhere on his car.

Ricardo squinted at me through the steam from his soup. "An explosive device in a vehicle suggests planning. Interesting. Was this lawyer a fed? I don't know him."

"He was a corporate lawyer, partner in a firm with ties to the people I'm working for on the Yap Island thing."

"The yellow diamond hustle," Ricardo said.

I nodded. "He was the attorney for Preston Pederson's company and he was involved in the Yap business because, without telling his partners, he tried very hard to get me to back off from helping Tod and Josie. Remember I mentioned that when I first got involved?"

"Sure."

"Okay. When he and I met, it was for lunch in a small downtown restaurant. The contact numbers he gave me did not include his office number. I have since learned that our meeting was not on his office calendar and his partner in the firm is not aware of that meeting. So my question is, was Anderson working off the law firm's books or was something else going on?"

"These aren't questions you expect me to answer, right?" Ricardo said, chewing now on a chunk of the cafe's tasty French bread.

"No, of course not. This is just context. So in that context, why was Anderson's car blown up? Where were he and his wife going? He lives out Minnetonka way. And my real question to you, given the circumstances of Anderson's death, is this: will there be a federal investigation? Are we possibly talking about a terrorist operation here?"

"Gotcha. Here's what I think, based on a couple of cases I know about and what little scuttlebutt I've heard. The state guys will routinely talk to the FBI and maybe the local CIA folks. Feds will probably determine it isn't a plot of international dimensions, unless they have something on Anderson or his associations. Then the state and Ramsey County or Saint Paul PD will treat it like any other homegrown murder, except for the explosive dimension, which puts it into a rarer category. They'll sort out jurisdictional stuff, maybe do a cooperative investigation. It'll all take time, and if it was my case, I'd hope the media attention would die down until there was some progress on the case. Like an arrest."

"All right, that's what I wanted to know. Thanks."

After lunch I called Mrs. Pryor to update her again. She made the appropriate appreciative noises, and I started staring at the wall. Pederson's funeral was the next day, and I hadn't decided whether I'd attend. Law enforcement logic and experience said perpetrators of heinous crimes often attended the funerals of their victims, but my sense in this case was that the murder was a professional job and, therefore, the shooter would be long gone and not interested in who showed up to mourn Pederson's passing.

The door to the Revulons' suite was closed and I saw no lights behind the rippled glass window, so I called instead of sauntering down the hall. Belinda picked up after three rings.

"I know I'm pressing," I said, "but I just wondered if you have anything for me."

"We're nowhere near done, Sean, but I can tell you there is an interesting thread that connects crime, construction, Chicago, Omaha, and Des Moines."

"Wow," I said.

"Yes, I thought so, too. We think we can show you a pattern of unindicted corruption in the construction projects these people were actively engaged in. There are political ramifications, of course."

"Do you have any idea when it started?" A little bell was chiming faintly in the back of my brain.

"Roughly seventy years ago is our educated guess. That's around the time two construction firms, one in Des Moines the other in Omaha, got started. That's also around the time a Pederson appears on the board of directors of the Omaha firm."

"That wouldn't happen to be Preston's father, would it?"

"You get the prize. There's more to do so hang up now, Sean."

I did. The sound of the little bell had become a loud clangor.

Chapter 31

I WAS READY TO DRAW a preliminary diagram of the case. It was something I started doing a few months ago on earlier cases. A diagram of connections between the preliminary suspects in the case sometimes suggested unanswered questions or questionable connections. Now, with the help of the Revulon cousins, I could see I needed to devote some attention to the Hillier-Anderson-Iowa-Nebraska axis. I hoped I wouldn't have to go there. I didn't like being out of town. I never took out-of-town cases. Well, almost never. Just like I didn't do divorce or tangle with the mob or international thugs. Ever. Well, almost ever.

But I had to figure out exactly how two Des Moines and Omaha construction companies actually got involved with the Twin Cities, so I had to do some research. I didn't have any serious contacts in the trades nor in the construction business so I thought about the possibility of documents, law enforcement contacts, or maybe friends who might know anybody or have any cases that involved the kind of malfeasance I was working with here. Then I had an idea. I called my friend Hector Eduardo Martine. Martine was a former construction boss with one of the largest developers and construction companies in Minnesota. Naturally, he wasn't in. I left a message and went back to my diagram.

My diagram expanded over several sheets of paper and I figured out, after inserting a few dates from my notes of earlier interviews, that the Pederson construction company had its genesis between 1945 and 1950. That would've been about the time Josie's father returned from military service. I needed to find out if he had been in the Pacific Theater. It might also help to know what branch of the service he was in. I decided I could do a little Internet research on my own. It took a while but I found a site that could give me some information about military units and their assigned service activity, if not about individuals.

My notes from interviews early on with Josie and Tod gave me his branch of the service and his unit assignment. There was some vague recollection in my fevered brain that he'd served in the Seabees and had been mustered out sometime in 1946. My recollection was correct and with those bits of information I did a few productive searches on the aforesaid Internet. I discovered his unit had indeed been in the South Pacific and, furthermore, he would have been released from active duty early in 1946.

The strands of the web were growing thicker and more securely attached. While I stared at my papers, I could begin to see a conspiracy that began with the discovery of precious stone smuggling to the U.S. from the Pacific Theater, the creation of a pool of cash used to establish a construction company in each of the cities to the south of me, and the periodic need for more cash. How to get that?

Ah, my imagination suggested, *suppose there existed somewhere a stash, not of cash, but of gemstones? And suppose during early struggles of the construction companies, when an occasional infusion of money was required to stay afloat, two trusted employees are dispatched to the stash. They discreetly convert the gems to cash, which could then carefully be inserted into the businesses?* That could explain certain undocumented absences by Messers Anderson and Hillier. Who better than a trusted though corrupt lawyer and his bosom school buddy as a guard to carry out such a task? I assumed the two had probably moved the jewels to Europe—Antwerp, perhaps, because I had read somewhere that there was a lot of diamond business in Antwerp. There's a lot of diamond traffic in New York City, too, but Antwerp was farther away.

And who better to help load up the supply chain with additional rocks than an officer of easy morals named Captain Richard Amundson, who just happened to be related to the founder of Pederson Construction? Once Tod and Josie began to do the research to find their long-lost granduncle, some people got nervous and decided to erase some links in the chain. Links named Stan Lewis, and Gareth Anderson and Preston Pederson. Never mind the collateral damage. Reluctantly, I decided I had to go to Des Moines. With luck, I wouldn't have to extend my travel to Omaha.

* * * *

I DIDN'T HAVE any current contacts in Des Moines. There was no one I could call to do needed legwork and an interview or two. So in spite of my aversion to highway driving, and no backup other than my trusty .45-caliber in the special harness under the dashboard, I made the four-hour drive to the capital of that grand state, Iowa. No jokes.

I booked a room at Mr. Carlson's Country Estates. Sounded impressive, but it was just a nice motel, located a couple blocks off Highway 35 in West Des Moines I wanted to eyeball the situation firsthand. Mr. Carlson's hotel was actually in Clive, a suburb of the city, just a mile or so from the location of the construction company offices that was my target. I was well-positioned to move on to Omaha, should that be necessary.

I had dinner, checked in with Catherine, and had a restful night. I ate breakfast in the morning and sortied off to Pellegrino Development and Construction. I had no expectation of finding anyone in the office who could help me. Indeed, when I'd called the morning before I drove down, the man on the telephone, with the vocal mannerisms of a relatively undereducated fellow, suggested I call the home office in Chicago. He further intimated I wouldn't be especially welcomed at the construction office.

He was right.

When I walked through the door marked PELLEGRINO CONSTRUC-TION, I entered a bright, cheerfully painted office of yellows and whites, a desk with the usual office equipment, and a pleasant looking young lady who smiled up at me and said, "Good morning. You must be Mr. Sean?"

Now, I had no particular basis on which to judge whether the woman seated there was a lady or not. Nor had I any particular basis for her instant identification of myself. That was mildly concerning. I raised an eyebrow and said, "And good morning to you. How is it you're able to so readily identify me?"

"You look a lot like your picture?"

Her smile disappeared, and she flipped over a sheet of paper which turned out to be a picture of me attached to my name and essential facts. I recognized the picture as one that must have been taken during one of my visits to the White Bear Lake home of Josie and Tod Bartelme.

"I wonder if Mr. Anderson is available? I would have called to make an appointment, but my time is short, and I just have one or two questions." I figured this Anderson might or might not be related to the deceased lawyer, Gareth.

"I'm sorry, Mr. Anderson is on a construction site downtown? I don't expect him until late this afternoon—if at all today?"

"I see. Then how about Mr. Hillier?"

The woman frowned. "I don't believe I recognize that name. Mr. Hillier?" She slid open her lap drawer and ran a well-manicured finger down a list of names in a small three-ring binder.

"I don't think that person is employed here, Mr. Sean?"

She was being so polite and deliberate, my teeth were starting to hurt. A good job of pretend cooperation. I wondered if she'd practiced saying my name out loud. Her habit of making almost every sentence a question was also getting on my nerves.

"Might I ask, is your Mr. Anderson related to the Anderson in Minneapolis? The one recently murdered?"

She blinked twice and said, "Oh . . . well . . . I really don't know. Murdered, you say? Oh, dear."

A few more minutes while she parried my probing questions with negative responses. Seeing no hope of a negotiated breakthrough, I thanked the woman and left the office.

In the car I contemplated my dusty red tennis shoes for a few minutes. Then I went back into the company office, moving as rapidly as possible without actually running. As I cracked the inner vestibule door, I could hear the woman on the telephone.

"Yes, sir. He was just here and I told him you were on a site in town."

A pause while she listened. I listened, too.

"No, sir, I said exactly what you wanted me to tell him. Oh, and he asked if you are related to an Anderson recently killed in Minneapolis?" There was a response and then she hung up the phone. I pushed the door wide and grinned at her consternation.

"Thanks for your help," I said and wheeled around and trotted out of the office. I leaped into my trusty Ford and wasted no time roaring out toward downtown Des Moines.

I reached the Pellegrino construction site. It was relatively easy to find, since my list of Pellegrino jobs had only a single Des Moines address. A large sign announced a high-rise retirement home under construction. I circled the block until I spied the wide gate in the wire fence that wound completely around the block. Parking inconspicuously down the street, I waited. In about five minutes, a dusty, black Lexus SUV with illegally tinted windows rolled out of the gate and turned east. I took a picture of the rear license plate as the vehicle disappeared down the street and then slid down in my seat to wait, propping my red Keds on the passenger seat.

Several hours and a bad taco takeout later, the site began to shut down for the night. I slid out of my vehicle and stretched. Two construction workers ambled by me heading for a local bar, if their conversation was to be believed. I saw no reason not to believe them. So I ambled along about half a block behind until I saw them enter a corner bar. I'd give them time to slake their thirst before making an approach.

I went into the bar, identified the two men and slid into an empty booth across the room.

CHAPTER 32

M Y PLAN FOR DES MOINES was to scratch around in the Pellegrino Construction Company and see what might reveal itself. If this Anderson, head of Pellegrino, was related to the lawyer Gareth, it might be easier, but that was an unknown. Neither my nor the Revulons research had revealed a family connection, but that didn't mean there wasn't one. I hoped I wouldn't have to spend another whole day in Des Moines. Maybe the two construction fellows would provide some substantive information, so I sat in the seedy bar and sipped a glass of beer the obliging black-haired waitress brought me. After what I considered an appropriate wait, I stood and sauntered to the bar where my two targets were seated side by side, engaged in earnest conversation.

"Gentlemen," I said, "might I buy you another round and in return have a little conversation?"

The men glanced at each othe. The blond said, "Sure you can, but I've seen that movie."

"Which movie would that be?" I riposted.

"The one where whatsisname," he rapped his knuckles on the bar, "yeah, Humphrey Bogart talks to some guy."

"*The Maltese Falcon*?" I wondered, gesturing to the bartender. The blond shrugged.

I suggested we move to a booth, but neither man was willing so I stood behind and a bit between them. Not ideal for a detective like me who put a good deal of weight in the interpretation of body language, facial expressions, clues like those, but I could be flexible. I make do with what's available. The workers' names were Bill and Bob. Bill talked some and Bob grunted. After we established some sort of basic rapport, I learned almost nothing until I whipped out two pictures I was carrying, one of Gareth Anderson, the other of Hillier.

Both pictures elicited a positive response. Yes, both men had been seen occasionally around Pellegrino sites or in the construction office. No, not recently. No, they didn't know the name of either. Finally, after a couple more rounds, Bill volunteered the information I should talk to a former employee of the company, a woman named Mary Astor.

"Seriously?" I said.

Bill looked at Bob, then at me. He squinted. "You think I'm lyin'?"

"No, no," I said. "I'm just surprise at her name. It's the same as a famous actress."

"Yeah?" Bill breathed. He hadn't made the connection, maybe never would. Mary Astor played a principal role in *The Maltese Falcon*, the movie based on the famous Dashiell Hammett book by the very same name. The two men looked at me and nodded wisely when I imparted this information. I paused and sipped my beer.

Bill told me, in response to other questions, that Mary Astor lived in a retirement home in the northern section of the city and had been a longtime office manager for Pellegrino. I should talk to her. Bob grunted his agreement. A lead. I bought my construction pals one more round and departed. It took me no time at all to locate the address of the Peaceful Retirement Home.

I was soon wending my way through traffic toward the establishment, which turned out to be a sizeable multistory building wrapped around a large, flourishing garden, which had been built on the roof of the parking garage which served the retirement home and nearby businesses. A call brought quick acquiescence from Ms. Astor to see me in the garden, where she habitually sat in the late-day sun for a half-hour or so when the weather was nice.

I went in through a lackadaisical security routine and entered the garden. There she was. Mary Astor was a short, spry woman of uncertain decades and a no-nonsense attitude. Since she was long gone from the company, she had no particular hesitation at identifying the two men from the pictures I presented. Yes, she'd seen both of them periodically in the offices, usually meeting with the top dog. That was her label for him. They were obviously not construction workers. She opined they might have been lawyers or politicians. They came and went together the half-dozen times she'd encountered them. Carrying briefcases, yes. Their attitudes and demeanors had been neutral, as if what they were doing was routine. The only reason, Ms. Astor told me, she remembered them at all was that they were among the few men who came to the offices who had no apparent connection to the firm.

I knew in my bones I was following the right trail. Anderson and Hillier were the couriers who carried illegal gems from a secret stash in Iowa to buyers in Europe. I was digging into something serious here, and it was making me just a bit nervous. Since it was now late afternoon, I decided to return to the motel for the night. When I entered the room, my perimeter meter flashed, the one in my head that said something was not right. I spent several minutes looking and couldn't find anything out of place or any traps like a listening device. Still, I might have missed something. I packed and settled my bill and departed Mr. Carlson's fine establishment.

Some hours later I checked in at a downscale motel in a small town in northern Iowa, just south of the border with Minnesota. I had been at pains to be sure I wasn't followed, jumping red lights, abruptly exiting the freeway, reversing my direction, putting on a long-billed ballcap, all the little tricks I'd learned to confound pursuers. I never saw any, and it may all have been a waste of time, but I felt better. I was alone and had lost any possible hounds sniffing along on my trail.

Mid-afternoon the following day I arrived home to the waiting arms of Catherine Mckerney. As I explained to her while settling on the couch holding a glass of very good scotch, Mary Astor had confirmed one other useful piece of information for me. The Anderson now running Pellegrino Construction was the nephew of the deceased attorney, Gareth Anderson.

CHAPTER 33

T HE NEXT MORNING I called Tod and reported I had new information and would have a report for him soon. I wasn't in the habit of making progress reports to clients, but somehow in his case, I'd fallen into that routine. "Have you settled on a new lawyer?"

A long sigh. "We've talked about it. Josie is very upset over Mr. Anderson's death, almost as much as about her dad."

"I'm assuming you're both still interested in getting to the bottom of the sabotage, yes?"

"Absolutely. I guess we may have to postpone a trip to Yap until next year. Sorting out the estate and the wills is going to take some time."

"You did say wills? As in more than one?"

"At least two, maybe three. There's Josie's dad's will, of course, and it turns out Gareth Anderson's will mentions Josie's dad and Josie, as well as his wife. Then there's his—Anderson's—wife, and I have no information about that."

"Do you have any information on who handles Gareth Anderson's estate?" His lawyer, if he had one, might have useful information. Tod didn't know.

After I hung up, I thought about these new complications. *Wheels within wheels. You smuggle a few pebbles into and out of the country and things get dicey.* I decided to call Mrs. Pryor. She was interested in what I had to say, but had no helpful information or ideas except the obvious: lay hands on Richard Hillier. So I went looking.

Naturally, Mr. Hillier was not to be found at his apartment in North Saint Paul, at his office inside Pederson Investments, nor working out at his athletic club, or anywhere else I tried. He was probably lying low. I thought him a likely suspect for the bombing of Anderson's Caddy, and the more I thought about it, in spite of his long association with Preston Pederson, if he could kill his school buddy, Anderson, it wouldn't be a stretch to find him guilty of offing Josie's dad as well. He would be severing any links in the smuggling chain that wandered from Southeast Asia to construction operations in Des Moines, Omaha, and Saint Paul. I wondered if there remained a supply of uncut stones stashed in some bank vault that Hillier could go for. I didn't see any way to acquire that knowledge short of torturing him, even if I had someplace to put him. Hillier didn't strike me as the kind of guy who'd surrender or give up any information, even if captured and sequestered. And that assumed I could get my hands on him in the first place.

* * * *

IN THE MORNING we caught a break. Or a break-in. From my contacts in the Minneapolis PD, I learned that somebody had tried to enter the home of the sadly deceased attorney, Mr. Gareth Anderson. Whoever had tried the surreptitious entry had seriously bad timing. While he crawled through a window on the west side of the house, a meandering cop drove by and saw the action. When he turned on his lights and fishtailed his vehicle to light up the side of the house, whoever was partway through the window abruptly gave it up and hauled ass out the back way. It was dark in Anderson's neighborhood, and though the cop gave chase, he never again laid eyes, or hands, on the would-be burglar.

The cops in Minnetonka put it down to attempted burglary, probably by somebody who read about the deaths of both former occupants of the residence. They assumed it had been an interrupted crime of opportunity. Maybe, but I wasn't so sure. If, as I still assumed, some diamonds still lay around, somebody from Pellegrino might be anxious to lay hands on said stones before a wandering estate attorney traced a bank account back to the wrong people. An account with a deposit box containing smuggled gemstones would be a distinct embarrasment. That evening I laid out my reasoning for Catherine.

"You're assuming there's still some smuggled loot, correct?" Catherine giggled at the old-fashioned gangland slang. Her occasional use of such street language did not fall as pearls from her lips. Still, I thought it was cute.

"Correct. But we better start with the presumption my idea's way off base."

"It's pretty bizarre. Hillier and Anderson have for years been funneling cash from stolen jewels into the business."

"Yeah," I said sourly. "If it's true, it shows a lot of patience and discipline. That's pretty unusual behavior. Though nothing about this case has turned out usual, so far."

"What you need is to track the handling of the Andersons' estates and how it connects to Josie and Tod, right?"

As usual, Catherine was putting her finger squarely on the essential piece.

"And the other avenue you might explore is that attorney's partners."

"Hillier." I ingested a healthy slug of scotch. "Hillier has to know something about all this. I'm still betting he went with Anderson to retrieve and sell the smuggled jewels. The problem is I have no way of coercing the information out of him, even if I can put my hands on him."

"Seems to me that's becoming more and more remote, yes?"

"Yes," I agreed.

"If you're right and Hillier is really just hired muscle, he's lost two of his patrons, in Josie's dad and Anderson. I'd not be surprised to learn that he doesn't have access to the stash of jewelry that you assume is out there somewhere. I'll bet somebody like that is probably going to run short of cash before too long."

"You are right, as usual," I said. "That's why I won't be surprised to learn he was the interrupted burglar. Somewhere, somehow, I have to acquire more information about Hillier's odd absences. Or about the good lawyer's. Where did they go when they went? Whom did they contact? How did they travel?"

"If they expected to get the maximum benefit from the jewels, they'd want things to appear legit, right?" Catherine frowned at her tablet. She'd recently bought another electronic toy. Meanwhile, I was still struggling to remember to recharge my new cell phone.

"Sure, but what's your point?"

"If they were taking jewels out of the country, to Europe, say, wouldn't they have to declare them? And didn't they fly?"

I could see where she was going with this line of reasoning. "Sure, and there must be some records somewhere. Probably in plain sight," I said. "Since it wasn't a big deal on the surface, there would be no reason to hide those trips."

"Hunting trips." Catherine smiled down at me. I was sprawled on the carpet at her feet where she lay on the sofa. Across the room, on the TV the evening news had ended and some guy with his arm around a black lab was going on about the upcoming hunting season.

"Fishing trips," I said. "Even today, crossing into Canada through the Boundary Waters or along the Montana border wouldn't be particularly difficult if you knew what you were doing."

"If the attorney—Anderson? Is that his name? If he did something like that, there's probably a record in his office."

I nodded and finished my scotch. "Correcto. There won't be a calendar entry that says 'diamond smuggling trip to Montreal.' But there will be something. And since the good lawyer is now, sadly, deceased, those records are likely to be somewhat more accessible." This might just be the wedge, the notch, the loose panel I needed.

CHAPTER 34

R ICARDO, MY FRIEND."

"Your timing's bad," growled my favorite investigator in the Minneapolis PD.

"My timing's off? For what, pray tell?"

"We're in the midst of a little kerfuffle here. Not your concern, but I can't talk with you right now unless you're confessing to one of our unsolved murders, or something equally world-shaking."

"Gotcha. Call me when you can."

Later that day we connected. By then the air conditioning in the building had completely malfunctioned. Those of us on the upper floors were in considerable discomfort. Outside, a relentless August sun beat down on the sidewalks and roads, and the fresh morning breeze had long since blown off down the avenue. It was hot in the city and tempers were undoubtedly nearing lift-off.

"I have a few minutes. What do you need?" Ricardo didn't sound amused.

I shifted in my chair, peeling damp slacks away from my inner thighs. "I assume you have in evidence various materials from the office of the deceased lawyer, Gareth Anderson, as your investigation into his death continues."

"I believe that to be the case." His voice had become flat, neutral.

"I detect a certain caution or hesitancy in your normally vibrant tones." I grinned at the telephone for no discernible reason. My feet, inside my red Converse Keds tennis shoes, were sweating.

"That would be affirmative," Ricardo said.

"Is that because you're being observed or overheard, or is there another reason?"

"Let the record show that the subject declined to answer."

"Now we're sounding like a TV show. A bad TV show."

After a moment of silence, Ricardo murmured, "We do have a quantity of stuff forensics are sifting through. Why?"

"If you have an opportunity, a quick look through Mr. Anderson's day planner would be mighty helpful, both to me and your investigation, as well."

"It's not my investigation, but I'll see what I can do. Can you be more specific?"

"Yep. Last year. Gap of a week or ten days in which he appears to be absent from the office. Probably with no explanation."

Ricardo grunted and ended the connection.

Days later, I visited Gareth Anderson's law firm.

A different woman sat at the front desk when I breezed in from the dusty parking lot. "Hi there," I said with a big smile. "My name's Sean. What's yours?"

"Eloise," she responded. That often happens if you catch basically good people unawares. "How may I help you?" She seemed nervous. One hand was out of sight in her lap. I wondered if there was an alarm button close by her fingers.

"I'd like a few minutes with Mr. Larson, if he's available." I smiled. Sweetly, I thought.

"Do you have an appointment?"

I thought I likely would've mentioned that if I had, but never mind. "No, I just popped in with some urgent business regarding your late partner." She looked blank. Maybe she didn't know about Gareth Anderson's recent death.

Down the short corridor a door opened, and I heard hard heels striking the tiled floor. They came our way. The woman who appeared, holding a yellow file folder, was the woman who had been sitting at the desk the last time I was in that office. She stopped short when she saw me.

"Oh, I'm sorry. Mr. Sean, wasn't it?"

"Yes, and it still is. I wonder if I could have a brief word with Mr. Larson."

"I'm afraid he's tied up at the moment. Perhaps I can help. Won't you come this way?" She turned—Ruth, that was her name, I remembered.

I followed her nicely shaped form down the hall to the same office from which she had just come. Inside I recognized a scene of disorderly reorganization. Lawyers' boxes, the kind they trundled to and from courtrooms, were stacked against one wall. Two metal file cabinets, one with two of its beige drawers half open, stood against another wall. The small window in the corner had a piece of ill-fitting plywood wedged into the frame. The large wooden desk was littered with file folders and papers.

"Excuse the mess. We had a break-in last night or early this morning."

"Did you call the cops?"

"Of course. They've been and gone." I realized Ruthie was watching me closely, gauging my reactions.

"Anything taken?"

"We don't yet have an answer to that question. Perhaps you can tell me why."

"Why?"

"Uh huh. Why the break-in, and why are you here again?" She smiled, sort of. Her smile put me in mind of a barracuda.

"I'm trying to trace Mr. Anderson's movements. See if there's a discernible pattern. Do you have his day planner or whatever he used to keep track of his schedule?"

"No, but we have a master schedule on the computer that keeps track of time blocks. Not individual appointments or court appearances. You understand?"

I did. "Maybe we could take a look at it?" She frowned and switched on the computer squatting on a rolling stand beside the desk. "Did the burglar get away with much?" I asked again, mostly to keep the conversation going. Sometimes I would get a different answer to the same question.

Ruthie glanced up at me and sank into the desk chair. Her fingers skipped over the keyboard, and the machine made a faint groaning sound.

"I, well, I guess it doesn't matter, he being dead and all. We can't tell if anything was stolen. We still haven't been able to sort out all Mr. Anderson's—Gareth's—work product."

"Things in kind of a state? I can understand that. A real tragedy, his death like that. Would you find August of 1995?"

"That far back? I don't know if—oh, here we are."

I slid around behind her chair and peered at the screen. August 1995 was blank.

"Okay, now try April 1999." I kept my voice low and confidential. I was playing on Ruth's unsettled situation. I hoped I'd get what I needed before she remembered attorney privilege and client privacy and stuff like that.

Ruth's flying fingers brought up another blank page labeled April 1999.

"All right. Can we look at one more?" She nodded. "October 2007." We drew another blank. Abruptly, the woman tapped a key that brought up a generic system screen. She swiveled toward me. Our faces were close.

"What's going on, here, Mr. Sean? Why are you looking at those dates? Why was this office targeted soon after Mr. Anderson was killed?"

"Very good questions, Miss . . ." I'd noted she wasn't wearing a wedding ring but I didn't know her last name.

"Watson. Ruth Watson. I ask you again, Mr. Sean. What's going on?"

I straightened and stepped back from her chair. "Here's what I know and what I just confirmed. Over a period of years, your Mr. Anderson and a Richard Hillier seemed to disappear for a few weeks every so often. Those dates are the same months and years for both gentlemen."

"Which means what?"

"I think it means Anderson and Hillier were together each of those times, and it wasn't to play games. I think they were carrying out a special service for some clients, a service that may have been dangerous and just a little bit illegal."

I stopped and Ruth Watson stared at me, waiting for me to go on. In the silence we both heard the telephone ring in the outer office. "Is that it? Is that all you're prepared to tell me?"

I didn't tell her that was pretty much all I had. "Do you have any information on Mr. Richard Hillier?" I could see Ruth was recovering her office skills and sloughing off her recent vulnerability.

"We might. I'd require a quid pro quo."

I nodded. "I think I can assist you with the police investigation here."

"Since we have no evidence of theft of value, I'm pretty sure the local police will consign the event to a low priority list." Her lips twisted. "Assuming they even have such a list."

"I think you should suggest to your boss he contact the locals and ask them to talk to an investigator for the Minneapolis Department. The one you want is the lead investigator on the death of one Preston Pederson."

Her eyebrows shot up. "You think the break-in is connected to Mr. Anderson's client?"

"I'd bet money on it." It was worth noting she instantly knew Preston was Anderson's client.

Watson frowned and nodded. "Okay then." She picked up the phone and punched in 9-1-1.

While she talked first to the call center operator and then to the local cop house, I surveyed the office. Looking down at Anderson's desk, I saw the lap drawer was open, a several-inch gap. I shifted slightly to put more of my body between Watson's shoulder and the desk. With a pen from my shirt pocket, I slid wider the drawer of Anderson's desk. For a long moment I studied the contents. There weren't many items in the drawer: a couple of distorted paper clips, two roller-ball pens, an unsealed tin of Altoids, in the corners some lint and there in one of the small built-in receptacles, two dark-colored, misshapen pebbles. I didn't touch them. I just stared at them from eighteen inches away. They looked to be about half a carat each.

Ruth Watson replaced the receiver in its cradle. I said, "There are two pebbles here in the drawer. I'm pretty sure they're connected to Anderson's death. I also think they could be uncut diamonds. Don't throw them out."

Watson jerked around and leaned over the drawer until our heads were almost touching. "I'll be damned," she murmured.

CHAPTER 35

THE AIR WAS STILL hot and oppressive when I punched the doorbell. I was back in Deephaven, standing before the large front door to the Pryor residence. Mrs. Pryor was expecting me, and once again she opened the door.

"Good afternoon," I said. When I stepped into the front room, a wave of conditioned air greeted me. "It's a fine day, isn't it?"

"Come in, Mr. Sean. I'm glad to see you."

She led the way into a second room with large windows that faced a sunny lawn, backstopped by what appeared to be a thick growth of bushes and trees about a hundred feet distant. She gestured me to a comfortable chair, and I sat. Mrs. Pryor refreshed her mug of coffee after offering me one, which I declined, and settled into a matching chair.

"You said something about a final report, I believe."

"Yes, ma'am. Since you financed a good portion of my investigation, I owe you an explanation of the investigation itself and my results."

She nodded, and I launched into a recital of recent events, starting with my trip to Des Moines and the Pellegrino Construction Company. I detailed my conversation with Mary Astor without mentioning her name, or the names of the two workers I met in that Des Moines bar. Mrs. Pryor was interested. I could tell. There was a gleam in her eyes.

Then I moved on to explain that Gareth Anderson had been doing a number of things off the books, as it were, and behind the backs of his two partners in the law firm. His will had been probated and a bank account and safe deposit box opened.

"Anderson and his wife had no children, and the people at his firm can't find any living relatives so it looks like this is the end for this branch of the family tree."

"I assume Mr. Anderson had an attorney. Most good attorneys do, you know," Mrs. Pryor said.

"Yes, the senior partner at his firm handled Anderson's will. His assets went to his wife and hers to charity and her church. All pretty ordinary and mundane."

"Except?" she said softly, never taking her eyes from my face.

"Except for a few pebbles in a brown manila envelope in the deposit box. There was a slip of paper in the envelope. No note, just the letters M. P."

"Ah," she said. I had a feeling then that she withdrew emotionally. The feeling only lasted a few seconds, but it uncharacteristically alarmed me in a subtle way. I was tempted to stand up, but I resisted and kept my gaze fixed on Madeline Pryor's face. Whereas before I had seen what I thought were welcoming smiles in the small creases at the edges of her mouth, there now seemed to be a sterner look to her. Yet her expression appeared not to have changed.

"Have you reached any conclusion about that? Those initials, I mean?" She might have been asking if I wanted a refill to a cup of coffee.

"No, ma'am. They could mean almost anything. They could be a person's initials."

"Such as mine."

"Correct."

Madeline Pryor looked down for a second and seemed again to withdraw. Then she looked back into my face and smiled. "Well, I have a confession. A small confession. I don't know if those initials have anything to do with me. They could also refer to my husband, Max. Or to someone or something else."

"Obviously, but you have to admit it's a bit of a coincidence."

"I never met Mr. Hillier, but my husband's firm did have business with Mr. Anderson. In the early years, immediately after World War II, two members of my family returned from duty in the services. One, a distant uncle, was in the army, stationed in the South Pacific. I don't believe he ever saw combat but in some of his letters, he refers to having met an officer named Terry Amundson. In one letter, which I still have, he called him R. Terry. I didn't really know my uncle, and he's long since died. However, after the war

Max told me he occasionally would get to telling war stories, and one of the men he mentioned was this Amundson who, I gather, was sort of sketchy. He was never court martialled, but he was reprimanded a time or two. Conduct unbecoming an officer, for example. Reporting late, things like that.

"When Tod and Josie told us they had been to Yap and were planning to organize a serious search for the aircraft Amundson had been on when it was shot down, we were of course interested. Max told me before he died that he thought Josie's father, whom he never got on with, was a reluctant backer of the project. Mr. Pederson put up some money, but he kept telling Josie and Tod to be careful. He seemed overly worried about their safety. We all put it down to a father's natural instincts, but it's now clear he didn't want the body or the plane to be located. We couldn't figure out why."

"He was afraid if they found the plane, they might also discover items that should not have been in the plane," I said. "Specifically, uncut jewels. Like these." I took a small white envelope from my shirt pocket and spilled three small pebbles into my open palm.

Mrs. Pryor looked down and poked at the gems with one slender, well-manicured finger. She sighed softly. "Yes, these look just like the uncut diamonds I saw at my jewelers. A little dustier, perhaps."

"These are most likely smuggled. I have to return them to the bank from whence they came. But I wanted you to see them because they represent a part of what this whole caper has been about. There's also the possibility there is information still preserved on the aircraft that could prove embarrassing."

"To Preston, or perhaps my family?"

Quick on the uptake, Mrs. Pryor. I nodded and continued. "During World War Two, military traffic out of Southeast Asia was focused on the war effort. A lot of flights came in with only cursory examination and some smart folks realized that smuggling small stuff with a high dollar value was better than trying to get bulky drugs across our borders, although there was certainly some of that as well. I'm sure that a certain pilot, acting as a courier and a transporter of planes, was able to carry contraband into the country fairly easily.

"He probably did it mostly for hire. He didn't make a lot of money, but he also didn't have to deal with processing the jewels at this end. He apparently made multiple trips with gems, which were then hidden away to be used as needed for the operations of some construction firms in Illinois, Iowa and Minnesota. Later, Anderson and Hillier became the trusted couriers who took the uncut jewels from wherever they were being kept and sold them discreetly. The resulting funds were fed into the firms' operations. The extra cash apparently gave the firms certain advantages."

Madeline nodded. "I see. And you believe there may be evidence on the airplane that would tie the smuggling to Preston and perhaps others? Have you discovered where the gems were being stored?"

"Not for sure, which is why this mystery is still unsolved. I'm persuaded they are probably in Saint Louis somewhere."

"What about the wounding of that young boy? Calvin?"

"I think that was another botched attempt to place the family in such turmoil they'd forget all about Yap."

"Will you look for the jewels?"

"Until Richard Hillier is arrested, definitely. I don't like loose ends, and Mr. Hillier needs to answer for his crimes."

"If you find the 'stash,' as you call it, what will happen to them? The jewels, that is, if any are left?"

A thought wiggled into my mind that Mrs. Pryor seemed mighty interested in this sidelight. But I dismissed that thought and said, "I don't really know, although I think the government might show up in the form of customs and maybe the IRS."

"Is there anything else you wish to report?"

"No, I think that concludes our business, until Mr. Hillier is apprehended. I think Josie and Tod will be able to return to a relatively normal life of preparing for another trip to Yap Island to look for their granduncle, assuming they can secure financing. With no more interference."

As I drove away and headed to my home in Roseville in the hot afternoon sun, I wondered where Hillier had gotten to. I wanted to bring him down. He was a killer and needed to be stopped.

My house, having been shut up for several days, was stuffy and the cats were upset. They weren't hungry but I gave them treats and some attention and then saw to routines around the place. By the time I finished, it was getting dark so I called Catherine to say I'd spend the night alone at home.

Chapter 36

My instincts were out to lunch when I called her, because Catherine didn't pick up, and I didn't react. She said she'd be going home. Well, maybe she was in the pool or the shower. Neither was true.

It was dark and very early when my second line buzzed and flashed, which woke me. Very few people knew the unregistered number of that line. A few cops, my cyber specialists down the hall, and Catherine.

I fumbled the phone to my ear and rolled over to sit up on the edge of the mattress. I heard breathing, distant thumps, and a voice I almost recognized. The voice seemed to carry menacing undertones, but under the circumstances, that wasn't surprising. I hummed something soft and unrecognizable. No response. With the phone stuck to the side of my head, I pawed at my clothes and began to dress.

Whatever this was, it wasn't good.

Moments later, a sibilant hiss, punctuated by gasps, said, "Sean. Hillier has me."

Even with the stress, I knew that voice. Somewhere, Richard Hillier had laid his hands on Catherine and was holding her hostage.

Apparently she'd been able to speed dial my number on her cell. I listened harder. In the background, Hillier was talking. It also sounded like he was moving stuff around.

"This is silly," came Catherine's voice. "I'm of no use to you."

"Shut up, bitch. Cooperate and maybe I won't shoot you after I get clear."

"What's in the bag?"

His voice was suddenly louder and clearer. He must be right next to Catherine. "What's in the bag? Why would you care? What's in the bag is my passport, my personal stash of rocks, my code to the bank in St. Louis, and the gun I'm gonna kill you with."

"Have you ever really killed anybody?"

"Jesus. Why'm I talking to you? Yeah, sweetie, bombs and bullets, that's me. If those damn kids hadn't insisted on diving in Yap an' got her dad all worried, he'd be alive and we'd still be sittin' pretty." His voiced faded. He must have walked away.

Catherine muttered, "We're in Hillier's apartment."

I grabbed the other phone to dial 911. When it rang before I could punch in the three numbers, it startled me. It was Ricardo.

"Sean, we've located Hillier. He appears to have someone with him. Maybe a woman."

My heart was thundering, and I had trouble capturing a full breath. "I know. It's Catherine. The bastard's holding Catherine. What's the address?"

"I'm coming," I said louder, hoping Catherine might hear.

After scribbling the address on a scrap of paper and dropping the phone, I ran to the gun safe and grabbed my Colt .45 and a box of ammunition. Feet slid into shoes and I scooped up keys, ID, wallet, and bolted out the door. The address Ricardo had given me was a place on the east side of Minneapolis, south of Franklin. At 3:00 a.m., or whatever time it was, there was little traffic, and I sped through town hoping to not encounter a patrol car. I probably upset a few wandering dog-walkers as I screeched around corners and ran a red light. A block from the address a Minneapolis prowl car blocked the street, and I parked, jumped out and ran toward the shot-gun-toting cop, waving my ID.

The cop looked, nodded and pointed down the dark street. I turned away and he began to talk into the radio pinned to his shoulder.

Detective Simon materialized out of the dark and dragged me to shelter beside a fat elm. "He's made one trip to his vehicle, the car parked by the door with the trunk lid up. He must have restrained Catherine while he packs up."

"She called me, and she's sort of got him talking. I left the recorder on so you're gonna probably have a confession of sorts. What's the plan?"

"Wait him out and take him down the next time he appears."

"I'm gonna get closer. Maybe I can jump him when he comes out."

"Don't!" hissed Ricardo. "There are several cops out here with guns. You could get killed."

I ignored his warning and trotted silently across the street. It was easy to avoid the two dim streetlights. When Hillier appeared in the doorway dragging Catherine by one arm, I raised my gun. Maybe he didn't know we were there. Hillier pulled the door to the sedan open, and the cops revealed themselves. Two big spotlights and four pairs of headlights in a rough semicircle lit up the corner and the building entrance. A voice from a bullhorn crackled, then roared, commanding Hillier to raise his hands and release the hostage.

Hillier slammed Catherine into the open car door and reached to his waist. Catherine cried out. Hillier raised a pistol, and someone off to my right fired a rifle. The bullet caught Hillier high on his left shoulder, knocking him back. Hands tied, Catherine lunged across the seats toward the passenger door.

I wrenched it open and clawed at her, dragging her out of the car and onto the warm pavement behind the front tire. Hillier raised his weapon and fired into the empty front seat. Another shot rang out and I heard Hillier grunt from the impact. He took two staggering steps and crumpled to the sidewalk. For a long moment there was no sound, then I heard the shuffle of many feet as a squad of cops rushed forward and surrounded a prone and dying Richard Hillier. Ricardo's partner, Leon, reached me and said, "You're okay, right? Didn't shoot, right?" I shook my head, reached to help Catherine up, slid my arms around her, clutched her to my chest. We stood pressed together, sobbing with relief and trembling with the adrenaline surge.

I put my weapon back in its holster and covered it with my shirt. I untied Catherine's wrists, wincing at the red marks left on her skin by the tight cord. Uniforms and a couple of strangers in suits with badges prominently displayed walked by, barely glancing in our direction.

"Guy's dead," I heard. An ambulance, lights flashing, no siren, showed up and the routines of forensic detailing a shooting scene moved into high gear. Leon escorted us back across the street and outside a line of yellow plastic tape. I was having trouble walking normally. The EMTs gave Catherine the once-over and declared her good to go.

More police vehicles arrived in a steady stream.

"Go. Home," said Leon. "Come to the station in the morning to give a statement. Okay?"

I shook his hand and Catherine and I sat in my car, winding down, watching the circus of cops for many minutes until the shaking went away and I felt I could handle driving us to the apartment.

AFTERWORD

AFTER CLEANING UP the telephone recording I'd provided, the county attorney had what amounted to a full—if rambling and expletive-filled—confession from Richard Hillier. He and his buddy Anderson had indeed couriered and sold uncut diamonds that had been stolen and smuggled into the states toward the end of the Second World War. Hillier essentially confessed to killing Preston Pederson and Gareth Anderson and shooting at Calvin. Even though the man was dead, his guilt in all this was certain, which meant the danger to the family had ended.

Hillier's luggage had several pounds of rough diamonds, and Josie's father's will revealed a bank safe deposit box with a small fortune in uncut jewels, including a rare top-grade fancy yellow diamond. Its sale alone would secure Josie and Tod Bartelme's financial situation and pay for more diving trips to Yap, which they arranged and took as soon as they could.

Josie and Tod's most recent expedition had pinpointed the location of the bomber that carried Josie's granduncle. What new secrets might be revealed would wait for another season and another trip to the South Pacific.

Strangely, with the right wreck found, Josie seemed less interested in what might be discovered inside the shell of that bomber.

Tod and Josie explained all this to me when we concluded our business where it had started, in the shade of umbrellas on their deck overlooking a peaceful lake. I drove home through the hot summer afternoon to a cool gin and tonic and the love of my life.